Kettorah and the Autom scrolls of light

Part 1. The Separation

By Sandra E. Carter

Cover illustrated by Chris Hamilton
Concept, and illustration by Sandra. E. Carter
Edited by Samantha House

Back layout by Gauntlet. L. Carter
First published edition paperback © 2019
Thomas Carter Publishing ©
wwwKettorah.com
ISBN 978-1-9162876-0-0

*

In memory of my Dad Leonard Carter the storyteller and for my beloved Mom Viris Carter

*

A little bit of help for your journey...

Tali – Second
Hibb – Hour
Yante – Day
Ashshun - Night
Camala – Month
Luca – Year

Language of Kemi

Places & Cities

Aluke
(Ah-luke)
Anobi Mines
(Ah-no-bee Mines)
Aqualeena
(Aqua-lee-na)
Bernal
(Burn-el)
Camu hills
(Cam-oo hills)
Gep
(J-ep)
Kargel
(Car-gal)
Kemi
(Key-me)
Kianda
(Key-and-a)
Nu Jahari
(New Ja-har-ee)
Nu Oarren
(New Oar-ren)
Saggitta
(Sag-jitta)
Tau
(Tah-you)
Trigon
(Trig-on)
Volker
(Vol-car)

Names & Animals

Aja

(Aah-Jar)

Alakas

(A-lake-as)

Nyper

(Nigh-pur)

Shedan

(Shi-dan)

Ulowpillors

(You-low-pill-ors)

Kettorah and the Autom scrolls of light

Part 1. The Separation

By Sandra E. Carter

--- CHAPTER 1 ---

HIGH PRIESTESS AND NU OARREN

"I Aja Daktari avenge thee; you took away my life and tonight I will take yours." The high priestess stormed with rage across the misty morning courtyard clenching her teeth.

Bursting open the door of the Oni sacred priestess' chambers; she entered the room clutching the hem of her heavy gown. With an angry outburst Aja ushered her maids

"Fetch my robes, my robes!"

The priestess had not long returned from the Camu hills after spending one and a half lucas in cleansed worship, she was not concerned with any royal celebrations around the palace but knew that it was her duty to return to the Empress. The priestess had not yet seen the King nor Empress on arrival back to Nu Oarren but was anxious to do a new sighting for Subira.

The handmaids hurried around frantically carrying the magnificent green and golden embellished priestess robe. One feeble maid fell to her knees as she rushed towards Aja holding the Oni headdress and necklaces,

"How dare you drop my headdress, you dimwit" with her piercing green eyes the priestess yelled looking down at the cowering, frightened maid.

"Get up, get up before I send you to the dark chambers."

The maid stared at the menacing priestess; her eyes wide open with fear. She hurried to her feet in panic, begging for mercy.

"High priestess Aja forgive me, forgive me."

The group of handmaids looked at each other with silent terror and worked hastily to undress Aja from her ancient black, bulky worshipping gown. The priestess gave a sigh and in a vile tone she uttered the words

"you pitiful weak creature."

The nervous maid took the turban off the priestess' head and started to undo her thick white locked hair, which stopped just inches off the ground. The maids all recognised that the priestess was completely different than before, her simple graciousness nature was now covered with evil viciousness.

The high priestess was undeniably beautiful, her skin tone was of a warm brown hue. Across her left cheek dawned three circular scars, which appeared once she became initiated as a high priestess. Only the chosen priestesses from her kinsmen of the Camu tribe knew of their true meaning and their purpose. Aja was selected by the superior guardians of the fold of Aluke at seven lucas old to become the High Priestess of the city of Nu Oarren. A gift was given to the Royal seer, it would prevent her aging process like other beings; she would age gracefully.

Aja's sole purpose would be to guard the anointed Queen or Empress by gift of future seeing and spiritual protection from birth to death, to assist with the childbirth of heirs to the throne. Her abilities also allow her to see into the past of anyone's history from physical contact, but she cannot read their future. Her wisdom and knowledge were sort after so the guardians of Aluke gave her young seers to train within the Kingdom to later be dispatched to other lands and families. Aja's role was ranked one of the highest orders, anyone that wedded her would be placed into a senior position within the Kingdom of Nu Oarren. This honour was given to her fiancé Duke, he was privileged to gain a Royal position without any questioning. As a wedding gift, he was drafted into the position of Imperial Officer over the Royal army. Aja honoured her birth right with excellence as High Priestess Aja Daktari for over twenty lucas, but now something had altered her loyalty towards the City of Nu Oarren; something was terribly wrong.

The maids had very little time to prepare Aja for the monarch's assembly as the entire palace and citizens of Nu Oarren were summoned by the King for a special Royal announcement. As Aja was almost prepared, she ushered the maids to leave her chambers. From a distance the sound of the Royal decree could be heard and musicians from the different sectors of Nu Oarren assembled at the entrance of the palace. Distracted for a moment by the resonance of the rehearsal melodies, Aja snarled as she glanced towards the closed door then quickly turned back. Her eyes focused on something within her chambers, there in the corner of the room hovered a large gold mirror.

Her hands slowly guided the gold mirror across the room towards the centre of the chamber. It suddenly halted parallel to a small circular glass window in the wall, as it hovered above a wooden table, it began to vibrate frantically. Scattered around the table were various sizes of velvet bonded ritual scrolls. A dim sky-blue light emerged from the centre of the mirror and glided towards one of the scrolls, which was immersed in a jar of water. The faint light began pulsing then exploded into a fusion of colours, cocooning the priestess.

A figure began to manifest within the sphere of light, a frail silhouette of a male appeared, a voice calling a name echoed around the chambers as the form floated towards her. Just as Aja started closing her eyes in an almost trance like state, there was a swift, hard knock at the door.

"High Priestess!" called a guard "you have been summoned by the Empress."

Aja suddenly opened her eyes as the orb of light and figure shrivelled back into the mirror, the light lingered for a moment then disappeared. With her left-hand Aja fanned the mirror and it immediately moved back to its original position. Angry with the disturbance Aja spun around, picked up her bracelets and jewelled staff then left her chambers to join the Empress in her quarters.

--- CHAPTER 2 ---

THE QUARTERS OF THE EMPRESS

Empress Subira Solomon, adorned a flamboyant regal purple gown, jewelled with the finest diamonds and emeralds. Her crown and fine shell earrings were crafted by the goldsmiths from the tribe of the Anobi mines, their families were the smallest in size, the darkest in colour and they were seldom seen. Orders for jewellery were placed in containers miles away and transported through tunnels; this tribe ran a lucrative trading system. The scorching yantes kept their topsoil baron and by the ashshun changed their climate to sub-zero temperatures, these conditions kept the Melcap tribe safe from intruders and thieves. Over many generations they traded with the Royal families and other distinguished clients, this kept there civilization wealthy and able to pass on their skills through generations. After carefully securing her new shell earrings, the Empress took her time to fasten a newly crafted golden brooch of the Royal emblem to her gown. Her soft dark skin glistened from the oils of the wonda plant; its scent could be smelt from afar and only Royal blood had the privilege to use its nectar upon their skin. Subira was not only stunning but she served well as a compassionate ruler beside her King.

The quarters were full of exquisite flowers, gold glistened along the room which complemented the deep pink walls, fine fabrics, outlandish furniture and ornaments adorning the space. Suspended above the Royal bed was a portrait of the Royal predecessors of Nu Oarren. The Empress' ladies in waiting surrounded her and completed their final adjustments to her gown, insuring her tiara sat perfectly on top of her long black, locked hair. Beyond the door of her quarters, there was a Royal sounding of trumpets; announcing the presence and arrival of Subira's mother, Queen Adama.

The Queen's long red braids fluttered behind her as she walked calmly towards the quarters, along with the trumpet players and her male guards. Queen Adama observed the Trigon warriors guarding her daughter's door, these warriors were specifically selected from their tribe because of their tactical skills in combat and loyalty. The warriors were hefty in stature and their robust chiselled muscles were covered by silver-plated armour. With a familiar friendly gesture Adama nodded at one of the female warriors. Once more the trumpets sounded, and one of the ladies in waiting opened the door to the Empress' quarters to welcome the Queen.

Subira smiled as she saw her mother entering the room and with a gentle bow, she greeted her. The Queen curtseyed towards her daughter as she was the wife of the King of Nu Oarren, all subjects including Adama must bow before King and the Empress on arrival or departure of their presence. It is tradition in Nu Oarren that the Empress only becomes a Queen when she bares an heir to the throne.

The Queen sat beside her daughter while the ladies in waiting poured wine for Adama; carefully placing a platter of exotic fruits in front of them. Each maiden was handpicked from distinguished families to serve the Empress and higher elite maids were chosen for higher Royal duties. Subira admired her mother's gold and yellow embroidered gown and how beautiful she looked at the age of sixty five. Adama looked into her daughter's eyes and gently touched her face; softly kissing both of her cheeks, Subira smiled and returned a kiss to the Queen. They ate and discussed amongst themselves the engagement of the yantes events.

After they entertained each other with stories, the Queen's expression altered. She gazed at Subira and reached into her pocket; drawing out a green glistening bracelet,

"You must wear this leckon bracelet, it will protect you my child." Empress Subira gazed into her mother's eyes; uncertain of the exchange of the jewellery.

"My Queen pray why this?" The Empress glanced down at the bracelet

"Have I not been blessed with many lucas of protection from our priestess?" Subira sensed and then saw her mother's facial expressions change; deep distress rising upon her face.

"Subira!" the Queen said quietly, "listen! Listen to me carefully my child, this is a new dawn and era my child, things are going to change and as are!"

At that moment the priestess' arrival was announced. The door opened and Aja swept into the room, unable to finish what she had to tell her daughter, the Empress' mother swiftly closed her daughter's hand to conceal the leckon bracelet. As Subira's hand closed around the bracelet it instantly stopped glowing. Aja suspiciously watched the movements of both the Queen mother and the Empress sensing their secretive energy.

"Your Highness!" Aja bowed her head and raised it slowly questioning their postures, seeing if she could read what they were discussing on her arrival to the quarters.

"Aja, my priestess, it is good to see you, I hope that your time at the Camu hills has brought you the peace you needed, you have been missed my friend."

The priestess took a deep breath

"my Queen, Empress Subira, thank you for your thoughtful words and the healing time you blessed me with, all is well."

Subira smiled at Aja

"I have been lost without you my guide, we are so excited to see what is to become of this yante, come, come tell me what you see, come!"

The Empress beckoned the priestess to come forward, one of the ladies in waiting brought a chair for Aja to sit upon. Queen Adama deliberately coughed loudly holding her chest to distract Aja, a maid ran forward holding a goblet of water. Subira looked over to the Queen and realised what she was doing, the diversion in place gave her daughter time to hide the bracelet. Subira immediately dropped the bracelet into the top of her gown, hiding it from Aja's watchful eyes.

Aja sat down on the chair glancing at the ladies in waiting, she looked back at the Royal family and nodded

"I shall begin."

Empress Subira ordered her ladies in waiting to leave the room, once the door was closed Aja started the seer ritual. Her left hand slowly opened, beckoning Subira to place her hand in hers, holding onto her staff with her other hand. Aja began touching various stones on the rod of the staff which were placed in various positions for the ritual; whilst slowly closing her eyes. It had been a long time since the last time they were connected, so Aja had to ground her energy through the staff. While Aja was in the trance the Empress positioned the bracelet so that it would not fall out of her gown.

Aja almost appeared lifeless while she sighted, she murmured for a while then opened her eyes which had now turned stone cold white.

Her voice echoed around the quarters and both Subira and Adama were waiting in anticipation of the priestess' visions. Aja began to deliver her sighting

"I see battles, internal battles, there is a block, I cannot see." Aja's voice started to change, it amplified and became distorted as if there were more than three people talking at once.

"Tears, great tears will fall, two nations."

"There is a block, what unfolds is unclear, I see no more I see darkness open into light, flames, the noise, the ground opens, it's too..."

Aja began to sway about, she gave out a loud cry argghhhh, this alerted the warriors and they burst into the room

"Your Highness!"

"It is well Murrock, please, please leave we are fine Aja has seen the unseen.

The warriors left the room leaving Aja to reveal what she had seen. The quarters fell silent and Aja closed her eyes to awaken from the sighting.

"Interpret!" Shouted the Queen mother, "Priestess, what does it mean?"

Aja opened her eyes and glanced down at the floor. Subira stood to tend to her priestess, Adama quickly grasped her arm pulling her back down in the chair. Shaking her head Aja looked bewildered by the sighting

"It is one where I must consult the superiors, this sighting is different Empress and it's unclear, what I saw there were images and sounds, this troubles me."

"This trouble you?" Queen Adama rose to her feet

"This is not good enough! If my child your Empress is in any danger this must be revealed now!! Go, go Aja, go back to the Camu hills, speak to the superiors, they must have the power to unlock your blockage, this is of high priority, your life depends on this translation, your Empress needs to know what you have seen." Adama's eyes rounded in a fearful stare.

"Your Highness, I will do as you will me to, forgive me, I just could not see, I have never not seen your forthcoming steps."

Aja got up bowed and left with haste out of the quarters. As the door was closed both Empress and her mother were rendered speechless. Queen Adama broke the silence after a long-exhaled breath filled with fear.

"You must leave now,"

"leave mother? Aja has never failed in a sighting, maybe it is because she has only just recovered?"

"No!! Subira it is not so; you must leave now."

"But... but the monarch, my King, I cannot leave Nu Oarren especially this yante, it is our..."

Clenching tightly around her daughter's hand pulling her up from the chair,

"It is even more important because of this yante."

"Come, I will explain, but we must leave now before Aja gets to the Camu hills." Nervously

Subira stared deeply into her mother's eyes. Clenching her jaw Adama's voice quivered,

"My child it has begun..."

Subira dragged her hand away from her mother in fright

"What? What has begun mother, was it something to do with this?" Subira pulled the bracelet out from the top of her dress.

"Yes, no, hmm.... I will explain but we must leave now, trust me daughter."

Adama embraced her daughter in her arms; anxious tears trickled down her cheeks, tenderly she kissed Subira's forehead. Adama then called out to the door

"Murrock, maidens, be present."

The warriors entered the Empress' quarters, followed by her ladies in waiting, the door was closed immediately after as they listened carefully to the Queen's commands.

***

The necklaces and bracelets clanged loudly together as Aja walked hastily down the Royal majorelle blue and golden corridors, the palace grounds were now full of maids and servants preparing for the monarch's guests. The maids and servants scattered to allow passage to the priestess, no one wanted to suffer the wrath of this uncharacteristic mood change. As she marched through, her thoughts were still on the sighting, her gift had never failed her before, she had never been unable to read a vision, so what was this? Her green inflamed eyes pierced the air attempting to make some sense, an answer to this blockage. Aja summoned one of the servants; a scrawny looking boy walked towards her with a troubled expression.

"High Priestess" he nervously spoke.

"Prepare my transportation, let them meet me near my chambers"

"Yes High Priestess." The servant nodded, walked on a little then stopped and in an unsure panicking voice uttered

"High Priestess, where shall I tell them you wish to go?" Aja stared at him in anger, she had just returned and now she had to go back

"Camu,"

"Camu, High Priestess?"

"The Camu hills, ask me no more, now go!"

The shaken boy headed to one of the holding bays, climbed upon a flyer and shuttled off towards the dock where Aja's hover carriage awaited. As Aja walked down the corridor her thoughts went back and forth to the sighting and its significance, she repeated every word around in her head and what was foretold. If only she could find some kind of link to this puzzling vision before she consulted the superiors, was it that her gift had been blocked by them or was her gift weakened by her pain? Her jewelled fingers clagged together as she touched the palm of her hands and muttered under her breath

"I must complete what I started; he may know of this vision."

As Aja stormed enraged towards her chambers, she turned the corner and almost toppled a large vase to the ground; swiping her gown and knocking the base, two young maids saw this and were able to quickly grab the vase before it hit the floor and smashed.

--- CHAPTER 3 ---

THE PROPHECY

Queen Adama explained to the warriors and servants what was to be done. They gathered all Subira's clothes and hurried to pack them in four huge travelling cases. Subira sat watching everyone scampering around her chambers, it was as if she wasn't there. Her mother stood in front of her clutching her hands

"Do you understand my child? What you hold will change everything." Empress Subira nodded, her eyes filling with tears

"Yes my Queen, but what of my King, he soon awaits me."

"Murrock, send this message to the King," the Queen whispered into Murrock's ear, the warrior then left the quarters heading for the King. Adama sat down next to her daughter still holding her hands,

"You must never lose the leckon bracelet and once you leave the palace wear it around your right wrist at all times." The Empress reluctantly nodded and took the bracelet from her pocket, staring at it with fear.

Aja arrived at her chambers, she could still smell the scent of the wonda plant and feel the fading warmth from Subira's hands, for a split tali she glimpsed a vision of the Empress and the Queen sitting down.

"What is this I see for a moment and then nothing" in a rage the priestess opens the door to her chamber and slams it shut, startling a footman as he walked by.

Murrock arrived at the King's quarters, the royal guards had their swords close to their chest; prepared for any advances made by anyone or anything.

"I have a message for the King, from the Queen Mother"

The guards towered over Murrock like gigantic statues, their black armour bared the royal leaf emblem on the chest plate. Murrock looked straight ahead at the royal chamber's door, awaiting their instructions. One guard took a device from his belt and scanned Murrock from head to toe to check that her vibration was correct.

The energy belt moved up and down her body, it pulsed and made a high-pitched sound.

"Vibration approved" spoke both guards.

"You may proceed."

The guards moved away from the door, which opened automatically. Murrock entered the chambers and the door closed behind her.

King Javari Solomon now awake from a troubled sleep, stood alone at the window to his quarters; gazing out to the picturesque royal gardens of his kingdom. Nu Oarren was one of the largest cities of Kemi, it was a magnificent and breath-taking kingdom. The palace was sat on a great mount surrounded by forests and the flowing river of Ikediora and lurking in these waters were backtoo. These prehistoric creatures were gigantic in size with a long thick tail, they had three rows of razor-sharp teeth and their eyes sat on the top of their head; glowing reflectively in the dark. Although their smooth grey skin made them seem harmless, this was not true. If they were ever disturbed by an unfortunate soul falling into their water, they would be devoured within a matter of talis.

Huge stone walls protected the kingdom and royal family, the north gate was the main entrance to the palace and there were three other exits. In all four corners stood a grand tower, their surfaces were decorated by sculptures and carvings of past royal families, this majestic fortress could be seen from afar.

Connecting the main entrance to the lively city of Nu Oarren was a long stone bridge. At the access point was a flickering transparent force field gate that enabled the citizens to see the grand palace, but they could only gain entrance by authorization of the protectors. Encasing the main city of Nu Oarren and the opposite side of the palace mount was a great wall. This wall stretched for miles with only one access point which was also guarded by the protectors and gave the city it's notorious reputation. Javari was a handsome and noble King who took great pride in his position, he truly loved his empire. His reign covered two hundred provinces and cities and he worked hard with his government to create a democracy for his people across the lands, after facing many lucas of wars, he hoped for peace.

Prepared for the celebrations he was dressed in a leaf patterned purple tunic made from royal silk and over coat, from his smooth onyx skinned neck hung the golden chain of office, which was filled with precious emerald stones, upon his wedding finger bore a signet ring with the royal hallmark of the obadiah leaf and enclosed around his forearms were golden armlets from his fore fathers. His thick, black, braided beard hung gracefully towards his chest and at the tip of his beard dangled a small green jewel. His black locks wrapped high above his crown, elongating his head. He became King at the age of seven lucas after the disappearance and the unknown scribed deaths, of his father King Agu and his brother Rufus the third at the battle of Aluke.

Javari heard the footsteps of Murrock entering the room,

"What is to become of Nu Oarren?" the King asked then gazed back at Murrock. "Your highness, Queen mother Adama proclaims the prophecy from her guided dream has unfolded this yante."

The King spun around, knocking a glass of water to the floor, he was now fully facing the warrior.

"Where? Where is the Empress?" he demanded.

"Preparation is at hand, Empress Subira will be taken to Nu Jahri, as Adama bids permission to leave with her."

Javari nodded,

"Deploy the protectors they must escort you. Let the Empress know we shall rendezvous at the falls, Adama cannot leave with her daughter, let her know this as well."

Murrock bowed and left the quarters, the King called his guards to summon his nobleman.

Five men dressed in red tunics and turbans, wearing a sea of necklaces quickly entered the quarters, scurrying around like wild insects. Three of them carried scrolls under their arms, one carried a telescope, and another carried a red circular velvet container. These men were skilled in many fields of great and sacred science; geometry, astronomy, astrology and were selected as the finest graduates of Nu Oarren's temple of enlightened knowledge.

"It is time, Adama has heard the words" spoke the King,

"initiate the diversions."

"Yes, your highness, here; here is the key." The noble man opened the container, which revealed the key.

Placed in the King's hand was a blue ribbon which hung from his palm, but where was the key? The key's vibrational frequency was so powerful that it could not be seen by the naked eye, three of the noblemen swiftly left the quarters leaving two to take any more orders.

"Foruth" the King called, at once a guard entered the room.

"Position two more guards at my doors; do not draw suspicion, then you and Dacken come with me"

"Yes your highness" he replied.

Foruth left the quarters, jumped on a flyer leaving Dacken at the door while he summoned more guards.

Foruth sped round the corner of the corridor, slowing down before he drew too much attention. He stopped by a holding area and commanded

"Inspections, you two must come," two guards leapt on their flyers and followed him.

Foruth was the chief bodyguard so it did not seem irregular for him to request or demand guards for training drills or guard inspections.

***

Back at the Empress' quarters Subira was now de-robed and placed in a purifying circle. Her handmaids poured jugs of water over her head and rubbed oils all over her body. The Queen sat overseeing their every move.

"Make sure the oils are well spread around her body."

The oil was used to cleanse the body from any entities and clear her aura.

The maids nodded and proceeded, Subira's eyes were closed as she sat deep in thought. She thought of what would have been a wonderful celebration of her kingdom, to now fleeing the place she loved so much. Her mind moved to and fro, going over what had happened in the short space of time. The Empress kept seeing Aja repeating the sighting, her thoughts then shifted to what her mother had revealed to her. Subira was now detached from her reality and placed into an unknown abyss.

Outside the courtyard of Aja's chambers, two handmaids and a chauffeur sat waiting in the hover carriage for the return of Aja. The door opened and out walked Aja, her head was covered with a veil and she was dressed in white ritual robes, she mounted the carriage bound for the Camu hills. It would take at least a yantes journey, as the hills lay far past the Tau tribe province.

--- CHAPTER 4 ---

THE HISTORY OF THE TAU PROVINCE

The province lay between the mouth of the pink and green meadows of the Aceba valley and the great river Ikediora, which streamed past and far beyond Nu Oarren. It once housed thousands of families who lived a humble and peaceful life. With the fertile lands they were able to grow many fine crops and cattle that enabled them to be self-sufficient. They traded with other villages and cities but sustained their traditional customs by utilizing natural resources; creating magnificent hive shaped habitats, adorned with spectacular artistry that predated many of the tribes within Kemi.

In the centre of the village was buried seven large hollow rocks, the natives used small stones to strike against the rock gong as a drum, it generated mysterious vibrations that resonated through the kingdom and could be heard from afar. Other cities and provinces of Kemi also possessed these ancient drums, which were once used to communicate with each other, tribe to tribe. Only the elders from each tribe knew of the true origin, the reasons why the rock gongs were placed there and why they played a sacred role for their lands.

Surrounding the village burnt tremendous clay vessels containing the wonda plant oil extract, the aroma's danced in the ashshuns air which created an ambiance of tranquillity for the Tau tribe. Although they reared cattle to sell, this tribe were not meat eaters, their diet consisted of mainly fruit and a vegetable called ban root which was a Tau delicacy, these contained almost every vitamin their body needed. Women weaved beautiful baskets from the leaves of the ban roots and traded them across Kemi especially in the trading village of Bernal.

The national exercise and training style of combat was called cumamba, their flexible bodies allowed them to move with grace and speed when required. In the yante they used spears to hunt, their spearheads were carved from black jet rock, at ashshun they would dance by fire light from the clay vessels; celebrating their daily tasks and life itself. The elders would group together and point at the lari constellations; reciting stories like wise griots, making the children gasp and laugh about their history. The King of the province refused to use fashionable technology and disregarded any of his kin to trade their produce for useless objects that could jeopardize their culture. They had no enemies, but the coming chain of events would change everything forever. A war erupted between Duke, the Imperial officer of Nu Oarren and King Rais of the Tau tribe, this war was unjustified. King Javari ordered a truce with the Tau tribe and invited them to become allies to Nu Oarren when he first became King.

Duke despised the Tau tribe as they were a primitive civilization and saw their breed as something beneath him. He was infuriated that their tribal territory was abundant with great treasures and resources, but they dismissed their commercial value to traders and saw the gems as sacred rocks, using them only for agricultural tools and other household devices. The ancient scrolls stated that it was forbidden to remove any of the stones from the province as they were placed in a sacred geometry aligning with the lari constellations. It was said they also brought peace to the planet; no-one had the authority to take a single stone; King Javari forbade this in their treaty.

The power-hungry officer became overshadowed by greed and hatred. Duke demanded King Rais should offer part of his land and treasures to Javari as a gift for becoming their allies and protecting them for many lucas. Rais refused this unreasonable request for they had already traded the wonda plant and precious meat from their kaduko beast to only the Solomon family as a gift of peace, this enraged the officer and led him to forge a dishonest plan. Duke reported back to King Javari that the Tau King refused to be a part of their federation any longer. They declared war upon Nu Oarren and would now be in alliance with Saggitta. Duke's scheming ways of persuasion corrupted King Javari's better judgement as many lucas ago they fought battles with their tribe and he had lost family by their hands, so hearing this brought up deep pain and memories, which Duke knew it would.

Javari was also aware that the Tau minerals had great powers and in the hands of Saggittans their kingdom could be under threat, Kemi had felt the wrath of this King's greed before. He trusted his friend as they had fought beside each other and he had saved him from death, so King Javari had no alternative but to sanction the invasion and deploy his warlords. Noblemen of the state, counsellors and priests all agreed it was the right decision and that it must be kept from the citizens of Nu Oarren to prevent pandemonium. The warlords and troops were sworn to secrecy by the King's court. Duke along with his selected commanders and troops sat in the tetragon combat quarters planning the attack on the Tau.

One of Foruth's young recruits overheard the plot but was unsure what to do with the information. Lieutenant Sonkel, Officer Junn and General Bakko entered the room as the young cadet left for his barracks.

The Imperial officer flew to the Tau lands with his battle fleets ready to unleash revenge upon King Rais' rejection. That ashshun the Tau tribe celebrated the birth of a new Tau, the child looked different from their other offspring, which only increased their belief that this was the sign their elders had prayed for. The powerful sounds of the ketta drums harmonised with the dancing feet of hundreds of tribal warriors, which echoed around the province; sending the sweetest surge of love in the air. King Rais and his wife were delighted that their scrolls pronounced this birth as part of the prophecy, that this child would change the pain of the planet. While the tribe rejoiced, they were unaware of what was approaching them. As the fires from the wonda oil vessels bloomed like flowers, a screeching sound came from the skies and in seconds the province was bombarded by waves of rays from the Duke's artillery. The province became a scorching inferno; the forests blazed, and its beautiful blossom fell like rain. Families ran in all directions looking to the skies in disbelief of what was happening, they started to fear that this birth was a curse and had created this surprise attack. The Imperial officer and his ground troops landed upon them like a plague of vinok insects, they swarmed the beautiful lands unleashing their weapons. Some of the troops raided the enormous sheds that stored clusters of emeralds and Duke even directed the soldiers to take the piles of wrapped wonda plants. He looked around at the large seven rock gongs but paid no attention to them as they were dark and covered with moss.

Tau elders fell to the ground screaming in shock with what was happening. King Rais directed some warriors to take the women and children away to safety, he then ordered his warriors to attack with no remorse. Warlords savagely stripped jewels from around the neck of some Tau and beat anyone that attempted to fight back. Thousands of light spears soared across the dark ashshun sky, heading towards the troops. Tau warriors sprung out from ground traps, vaulting upon unsuspecting soldiers and slashing them with their war claws. Snare nets and ground traps were used to capture many of Duke's unaware men. Some of the troops were catapulted over the burning trees far into the forest. Tau warriors rode gallantly on the back of the anorda beasts, they ran through the battle fields tossing the enemies in all directions. The Tau tribe were unlike any other kin of the planet, they had more animal features and possessed a remarkable and unique gift which enabled them to shape shift into beings by the will of touch. Their skin was patterned with shades of green patches, which allowed them to have great camouflage in the forest. With creditable speed and agility, they outran Duke's men who were scattered violently and thrown to the forest floor, not knowing from which direction the attacks were coming from. Some of the Tau transformed themselves into copies of Duke's men, confusing the troops and enabling them to attack on many levels. Even the smallest of the Tau children gave attack to protect their lands and their home.

Some of the vulnerable villagers escaped and fled towards the Camu hills where they would seek refuge. A small amount of survivors, badly injured, dispersed deeper into the forest to lay in wait until the fleets left their land. They stood frozen in horror filled with vengeance and anger, tears fell from their eyes, their hearts and spirit now broken. Their home and kin lay dying amongst debris of flaming huts and undergrowth for what? All they repeated in their minds was that this must have been brought upon them, by the child's birth.

The Tau warriors overturned some of the terracotta vessels of wonda plant oil and ignited some of the ships and troops. The warrior's fought with great honour, killing as many enemies as possible, they battled for their kin and land. Horrifying screams of terror rose with the bellowing clouds of thick smoke from the battlefields, dampening the sweet odours of the serene land. The battle lasted for many hibbs; Duke was surprised at the power of these warriors, but their strength was no match for his warlord's weapons.

The Tau palace was demolished, instantly killing the King and Queen as they refused to leave their land. The troops were given the command to leave no survivors and they began herding those too weak to run and fight. Good fortune fell upon the royal children as they were rescued and carried away by their personal servants and guards. A Tau child baring the most beautiful emerald stone hid quivering under a basket off ban roots. The imperial officer and his guard heard the child whimpering and he turned over the basket revealing a little boy who was around four lucas.

The boy's tail swiped at Duke's legs, tossing him to the ground and muddying his long blonde hair and he bit the leg of a guard. As Duke scrambled to his feet, in embarrassment and disgust, he drew his blade and cut off the child's tail, this spiteful act would now prevent the little boy from ever revealing his true Tau form again. As the boy had touched the guard, he had transformed into a white skinned, blue eyed child, he was not strong enough to form a fully-grown man. Duke gasped, stepping back in astonishment, his eyes fixed on the boy mesmerised by the metamorphosis; he had heard of their abilities but had never witnessed it first-hand. The officer grabbed for the sparkling stone, but the boy held on to it with all his might, while crying in pain from losing his tail. Duke picked up the kicking and screaming little boy, handed him to his guard then gave a signal to his commanders to round up the troops and left to board his vessel.

***

Back at the trainee's quarters the young recruit sat riddled with guilt decided to inform the chief about what he had overheard. He requested to speak with chief Foruth who was seated in the tetragon combat quarters discussing the strike with other warriors. The recruit told them that the invasion was unjustified and that the Imperial officer had not acted under the royal decree. On arrival to the palace the guards and warriors seized Duke and his troops; they were taken to the dark chambers to be sentenced for treason. After all of them were tortured within an inch of their lives, the officer was brought to the King for his final last words.

The once sinister man was now begging the King to spare his life, as his wife high priestess Aja Daktari would soon bare their first born. Faced with disappointment, anger and the death of countless innocent civilians, Javari wanted to take the lives of all involved, war should not be provoked if there is no just cause. Duke had now created an enemy instead of comrades, this was a dishonourable violation of their laws.

Javari knew Duke from his childhood and could not understand the reasoning behind such spineless wickedness, greed had somehow infiltrated the blood of Duke and its venomous head must be cut off. The compassionate King granted his wishes not to kill him but as Duke's punishment he was banished from the kingdom never to see his wife or the birth of his child.

The King ordered that no kin of Nu Oarren should touch the ground of the Tau land, but to leave them to rebuild their lives. The truth was scribed and classified forbidden then sent to the Camu hills for protection. Defeated by the thought of such an unscrupulous act which could have cost Javari his crown, he had to continue fuelling the rumour of the war, that it was declared by the Tau King, there was no guarantee the truth would not be revealed one day. Their law stated unlawful killing could be trialled against the King which could lead to him or her to step down, Javari was aware that he might have to do this one day and lived with the guilt of trusting his friend and not seeing the evil which really lay in his heart. Some of the Imperial officer's troops escaped captivity and fled to the land of Kargel, they had within their possession the loot, some captured Tau men and women and the little boy with the emerald sparkling stone.

Word was later sent to Aja that her husband was killed in battle; she was devastated but Aja sensed the guards were holding something back, but she could not question the King's message of condolence. Hate towards the King grew, for if he had not sent her husband to war on the Tau, he would still be alive. Officer Junn the cousin of King Javari spent time with Aja before she left Nu Oarren again, he consoled her through losing her husband and even escorted her when she was given permission to leave. The priestess was then sent to the Camu hills to mourn; she soon fell ill from the death of her husband and was to remain there for a longer time.

--- CHAPTER 5 ---

MEMORIES OF A KING

King Javari stood in the quarters pondering over Duke and questioned if he was still alive and what sort of person he would be now. The noblemen unwrapped scrolls upon scrolls and plotted out the ninth star and the lari constellations, turning to the King in a pompous way he said.

"In four lucas your Highness the first two planets shall set the season of the north flame, then two more in the next four lucas shall set the season of the south land, the season of the west wind, the season of fluid law, then the final one shall rise when on the eighteenth luca. The name of this cycle is unknown, not even the priestess' or priests of the Camu hills know of this season, we sensed and plotted two different frequencies; one predicted the prophecy, the other we are not sure of where it comes from, we can only hope."

The second noblemen walked to the window pointing his telescope towards the sky. Javari looked immediately towards the pompous nobleman, hastily answering his abrupt announcement.

"Hope! Through perseverance, gives us faith and faith hope, I stand confident that all our tablets, testimonies, scrolls, guardians, griots reveal truth, hope, nobleman, hope."

The other nobleman quickly butted in to not upset the King any further, his voice quivered

"It, it will be more visible in the ashshun hours, your highness."

The King nodded at him then glanced at the now shamed nobleman directing his reply

"it seems all is not lost."

The door was opened and Foruth entered with Dacken

"Your highness the guards are in place."

"Come Foruth, Dacken, to the falls."

The guards walked towards the walls of the quarters, standing at each side of the wooden framed mirror, the King walked slowly towards the mirror, lifting the invisible key and pointing it at the mirror.

A lock materialised and once fully recognisable the King put the key in the lock. The mirror disappeared to show a tunnel. The King and his guards entered the tunnel, as soon as they crossed the threshold the mirror became visible again, leaving the two noblemen gazing at the closed entrance.

The tunnel was narrow and dark, it curved downwards around the building, Dacken and Foruth crossed their arms striking their torso firmly, their armour became luminous and this gave them light to lead the King to the falls and secret gardens, deep beneath the inner palace. As they marched downwards King Javari recalled his first experience of being in the tunnel.

***

As a young boy around seven lucas he was playing the game ouah orb with his cousins: Sonkel, Junn and Bakko. The game soon turned into a brawl as they always did when the four boys played. The game consisted of hitting an orb of light around different fields with gloved pads on their hands. His cousin Junn hit the orb at great speed, which hit Javari to the ground, Junn teased little Javari, telling him that he would never be King because he was not strong enough nor had not grown a mane of royal locks and he lacked tactical skills. The boys started wrestling with each other, Junn was much older than the King and quickly overpowered him and began pounding his cousin viciously. His other cousins Sonkel and Bakko laughed as they fought and blocked their fight from the maids.

The maids soon parted the quarrel and little Prince Javari was brought to King Agu. Wiping his tears and bloody nose, he told his father what his cousin had said. The King smiled and said to him

"My child your locks will grow and one day you shall be a great King, you will become strong. Inner strength grows when it is tested, you must learn to have faith my son, believe in something that has not been seen."

Javari wiped his tears and asked cheekily

"believe in what?" scowling at his father.

"Your cousins bring out the strength in you. You will thank them one yante."

"Thank them? Never father!" Javari turned his back to his father.

"Never turn your back to the truth Javari, stand in truth and stand in honour."

The King frowned for a moment, then turned to a container

"open it and tell me what you see"

Javari opened the container and there before him was a blue velvet ribbon. Unimpressed with his findings he screwed up his face then looked back at his father smugly

"a ribbon?" The King turned away towards the mirror and said,

"Look again my child."

The Prince peered back into the box, he stared harder this time and noticed that the ribbon lay in the box, but it appeared to be attached to something. The Prince then cautiously put his hands in the box and to his surprise touched something.

"What? What is it father? What is it?" pulling his hand back in fright.

The King looked down at his son and chuckled,

"it is a key, my son."

"But I cannot see it, but I can feel it!" Javari exclaimed

"Javari this is faith, you cannot see everything but something's are always there, you cannot see wind but by feeling the breeze on your face you see it is there, you can even hear it too, this key is very special, come." Beckoned the King.

Javari looked at his father puzzled by his riddles but followed him anyway.

Stroking his beard, the King got up and strolled over to the mirror, then handed the key to his son.

"Move it towards this point of the glass" he said pointing to a spot on the mirror, as the Prince did so a lock appeared.

"Open it"

A scared Javari pushed the key into the lock and to his astonishment the mirror disappeared revealing a tunnel. The King paused in the doorway of the tunnel, slowly pulling the key out he said to his son,

"never look back, advance forward at all times, trust your intuition for you will always find the light."

The King gently ushered his son into the tunnel, the door automatically closing behind him, leaving Javari in the dark, damp, mouldy space. He screamed in panic and cried out to his father and banged his fists against the mirror, he yelled but had no reply as the figure of his father began to fade. Javari sat down for what seemed to be many hibbs; crying and feeling abandoned by his father. Hate began to course through his veins, he felt that his father was mocking him just like his cousins do. His heart raced franticly as he tried to catch his breath, trying to be brave he slowly wiped his tears and got to his feet. With anger in his tear-filled brown eyes he stopped thinking about his father and focused on getting out.

Javari started to walk, touching the walls as he went, feeling the coldness and the damp moss that decorated the stones. Wiping his hand quickly on his chest he then put his hand before his face, but he could barely see it, his little body could not hold back his fears and a brassy tone expelled from him. The sound and smell disturbed the tiny taco bugs, they scurried in many directions to get away from the scent, even he was shocked at its odour and waved frantically to get fresh air. The taco bugs soon moved back in formation and gave him some source of light, he quickly noticed they were all moving together across the walls down the tunnel, using his intuition he followed them in the same direction. Javari shuffled down the tunnel slowly, using the wall as a guide, every now and then he sniffed to try and keep calm; fighting back his tears from falling. As he continued walking, he could hear water flowing, he paused for a moment and remembered his father's words of not to look back. Javari looked over his shoulder into the dark void behind him but quickly turned back and continued forward.

Step by step the noise of water became more apparent and a sweet scent wafted towards him, finally he saw a glimmer of light. Javari began to run down the tunnel as fast as his little feet would carry him; puffing and panting he wiped the sweat from his forehead, he just needed to get out. His thoughts raced and he shouted,

"I'm going to run away when I get out of here."

Just ahead he could see the bright rays of sun light beaming into the tunnel, Javari got to the end where he wrestled frantically through the hanging plants blocking his path and burst through into a spectacular garden. He gasped in amazement with eyes open wide he absorbed the splendour of this secret garden.

"Wow," he faintly murmured.

The sky was of an unusual silvery colour that shimmered and sparkled like crystals.

The garden had grown from a large sink hole and moulded over thousands of lucas, giving it time to grow. Beautiful and rare trees baring beautiful fruits, exquisite multi coloured flowers of various sizes packed the landscapes. The aromas enchanted Javari's senses as he closed his eyes for a moment to take everything in, the warmth, the smell and sweet sounds, he was amazed of its existence beneath the palace. There were extraordinary birds with colourful plumes that flew around the diamond sparkling skies, great statues of Javari's ancestors decorated the garden. A long waterfall poured down gallons of shimmering fresh water, running into a large pool that then disappeared underground. A mixture of rare wildlife peeped out from the bushes but ran away as they took sight of the little Prince. Nesting flufful flies decorated a swirling bridge that tapered into the waters like an optical illusion. From a distance he could faintly see his mother, Queen Charlotte sitting with her maids in laugher.

In front of him sat alone on a stone bench was his father

"What took you so long?"

The King smiled, beckoning his son to come to him, he ran over to his father as fast as he could, bursting into tears and clinging onto his father for dear life. The King squeezed his son tightly, then wiped his bloody nose with a handkerchief and spoke softly

"one day you will be a great King."

Queen Charlotte gave them a big wave as she saw them clutching each other tightly knowing that Raju was teaching him a life lesson. Javari tried to sit on the King's lap but quickly noticed that his father was turning his nose up at him while glancing at the stain on his trousers. Embarrassed by what he had done he fidgeted, trying to pull his pants from his sticky bottom. The King chuckled at the sight of his messy child and pulled his cloak over his legs then lifted him to sit down. He then calmly whispered to his son

"even when you do not see light in the darkness a breakthrough will come, darkness opens to light, but first you must understand that darkness has the power you give it, the stars cannot shine without darkness, so you must always aim to be brave"

Although Javari was seven lucas he understood his father's lesson and would never forget it. He remembered that evening his father bathing him from head to toe both in fits of laugher, King Raju wittingly took the embarrassment away from his son to now a family jest. Those were some of the last moments he shared with his father and treasured them dearly.

***

Dacken halted,

"we have reached the entrance your highness."

Both guards held back the hanging plants and King Javari walked through the opening, smiling while remembering his father's lesson and his mother's warm kindness, she had died four lucas ago, he erected a beautiful statue carved from her favourite tree to honour her. He strolled in the direction of the falls, instantly realising this was that crucial moment to use all his intuition and power. He was obliged to protect Subira at all costs, even to sacrifice his life, for the prophecy must be fulfilled in his lifetime. Once by the falls he sat for a while, closing his eyes to take in the warmth and tranquillity of the garden.

Back in the palace, the Empress, now fully clothed was making her way to the King, unlike her royal garments the gown she wore was plain brown, a large hooded coat covered her head. The only jewellery adorning her body was the leckon bracelet which dangled from her wrist and the royal brooch hidden away under the coat. The protectors escorted her along with Murrock and two handmaids. Queen Adama retreated to her quarters, as her work was done; what the guardians had told to her as a child was unfolding before her very eyes. Her beloved daughter Subira was the chosen one. Adama wandered around her room looking intently at pictorial holograms of her beautiful daughter, she came across one painting which brought a smile to her face and a tear to her eyes, Subira was delicately held by her father Leo-vin. Other images she viewed were of the Monarch's day, the day Subira was crowned Empress of Nu Oarren. Holding the painting close to her chest Adama sat down on her bed.

Troubled tears trickled down her cheeks it was out of her hands now, only the true pure guardians and the fulfilment of the prophecy could save her daughter now.

--- CHAPTER 6 ---

THE FALLS

The underground garden hid many secrets, the Royal family spent endless time preserving its beauty. Soft melodies of flying kuffa birds charmed away the anxiety and bought serenity to Javari's troubled mind. With his head resting upon a carved tree seat, taking in a moment of stillness he waited patiently for his wife. He closed his eyes and bathed in the peace and joy of what was to be, then his thoughts came back to a bitter reality. From a distance the handmaids entered the garden followed by Murrock, in between the protectors was his wife Empress Subira. As they embraced each other with a soft kiss, all the servants disbursed into the garden; allowing them time to speak alone. They ambled towards the falls; its purple waters glistened and sparkled like gems. Javari scooped up a bowl of water and offered his wife a sip. As she drank, her heart could not hold back her tears, he could feel her fears and uncertainty of what was to come.

"My love, Javari this cannot be, I cannot flee and leave you alone, what danger can we not face together, haven't I been beside you in many battles before? Mother speaks of the prophecy, but I don't understand how can I have been sheltered from all of this, even this?"

Her hand lifted the leckon bracelet and it glimmered, blinding his vision for a second. Javari gazed deeply into her teary sorrowful brown eyes.

"I cannot leave you, I cannot, I will not, I will not!" said the Empress bursting into a flood of helpless tears.

Javari held her tightly wiping her tears away; cupping her face with his hands he kissed her tenderly.

"Subira my love what we have will never change but this is different. You cannot stay, I forbid it! Your life is too precious to me, I will join you soon, the lari stars will not keep us apart, we had to keep this from you as Aja would have seen too much and for this reason you must wear this" he said holding her wrist that wore the leckon bracelet.

"How can you all weigh such a burden I me and tell me nothing like I am a child? This is too much, to say I have no protection from Aja, only this bracelet, this!" she wailed.

"Subira you were born for this very day, our blood lines did not meet by accident, it was written, I will protect you at all cost, this is our destiny. I promise you; we will return to a greater place; you must keep strength in faith." He comforted.

"Javari, I hear your words, but my soul is heavy with uncertainty, bloodlines? Lari stars? I have had Aja with me since my birth but now you all tell me to run away from her! Has she not gone through too much all ready? Knowing that she has no more use to me, so what does this mean to her life?" Her nostrils flared with anger overwhelmed with the feeling of not being in control of her life and worrying over her beloved seer.

"Don't my feelings and my say count Javari?" she questioned.

He just staring at her with his eyes opened wide

"no! Not this time. It is my duty as King and I ask you to obey your husband"

Javari's voice became stern, her brow sunk with sadness for she knew this was not a disagreement that she would win. With a shaky voice she raised her head, took a deep breath

"I will do what is asked of me, my husband, but know this I am far from pleased"

A sheepish smile spread across his face for she never lost their quarrels but this one there were no real winners. He drew her closely to him resting his chin on her head

"Gogo will protect you, she will explain to you when the time is right, I am sorry my love."

He playfully bucked his forehead on hers, a tiny chuckle escaped her as she knew he was trying his best to bring some light to her pain. Subira pulled away from her husband and faltered,

"It's just that, how can our lives be turned upside down so quickly, when it was going to be a wonderful day in our Kingdom, I feel numb Javari, numb this is happening too fast I just....!"

He squeezed her even more tightly and they stood still for a moment, no words uttered from his mouth. He took her hand and guided her to walk with him. The vexation gradually trickled away as she felt his firm protective grip, she knew then, that he was scared too but dared not to dishonour him by calling out his fears. Her eyes glanced around the garden then looked back at his worried face.

"I, I sometimes forget how beautiful our secret hidden gardens are" beamed Subira, he lifted her hand and placed a sweet kiss.

"Yes, my love but not as beautiful as you, you are all that is wonderful, beyond the lari stars cannot hold a vessel of the love that I have for you" he cooed.

Subira side eyed him at the words lari stars, he caught the gesture but chuckled as they carried on strolling. Dacken and Foruth came in their sight as they waited patiently for the King's orders.

They walked for a while around the gardens, knowing they didn't have much time left together; stopping by the monument of his mother, Javari gently seated her on the wooden bench, Subira rested her head upon Javari's shoulder wondering when they would be together again. Javari could sense her anguish and softly rubbed her arms, he then glanced down at her bracelet,

"we will see each other soon, listen to Gogo she will guide you, Subira you must be safe."

Once more they held a passionate kiss, neither one of them wanted this moment to end but this was the only way to save not only the Empress but their planet. Murrock walked back towards the royal couple as she saw Javari's hand signal

"your highness we must leave, now!" the King nodded, the handmaids and protectors stepped forward to accompany the Empress to her carriage.

Subira turned back which displeased the King, for his training did not permit that but he did not stop her, her arms wrapped around him stealing one more kiss, as she moved away the final touch from their fingertips was the last time she would hold her husband, when next she did not know. As they walked back through her entrance to the gardens, she gave a request to Murrock, the warrior then followed the King to give a message to the Queen from Empress Subira. They would rendezvous at the east gate away from the festivities to board the royal craft.

--- CHAPTER 7 ---

THE BANQUET

The grand palace was buzzing with activity; all the tribes arrived at the palace ball room, royalty from Skylan, Volker, Trigon, Gep, Kianda and other provinces, ambassadors from Nu Jahri, noblemen and women and selected citizens of Nu Oarren, all gathered waiting for the presence of the royal couple. Dozens upon dozens of servants moved in and out of the busy crowds, carrying trays full of the finest delicacies. The chattering of foreign guests consumed the atmosphere, there was an array of costumes and extravagant head dresses from the diversity of tribes which created a dazzling sea of colours. Scores of patterned bald women from the tribe of Gep ordained with colourful prints all over their bodies and beaded plates around their necks dazzled everyone. They entertained guests with their spectacular and captivating tribal dancing. Melodies from conco bells on their decorated feet echoed around the banquet hall, drumming tambourines and singing instruments brought highlights of magic to the ambience of the celebrations. The enchanting display of fessal dancers moved at great speeds on their toes, their orange costumes chimed like tiny cymbals. Cheers roared across the mouths of the distinguish guests.

The Royal flags were erected at full mast, displaying the Royal obadiah leaf emblem of Nu Oarren. On the balcony of the banquet hall, long large metal kakakis announced that the Monarchs had arrived, ahead them two great black alaka beasts strolled gracefully; male and female glistening with their golden chains, positioned themselves at opposite sides of the balcony. Standing regal in their crowns stood King Javari and Empress Subira, dressed in their royal gowns covered with their jewels, throwing up their hands the crowd erupted in great cheers, the kakakis blew again, clapping and joyful laughter engulfed the exquisite grand room. At the entrance of the ballroom stood a tall figure, their head and shoulders were covered by a golden decorative mask. The figure began to walk leisurely towards the balcony, their eyes fixed firmly upon the King and Queen.

Throughout the palace the servants rushed around into their positions to see what this royal announcement would be. One of the Empress' maids looked up at Subira, she whispered into a footman's ear

"I'm sure I dressed her hair better than that" she giggled,

"in fact, her brooch is on the wrong side"

"We will have none of your gossiping maid, just be quiet!" the footman laughed.

A few steps away overhearing their conversation was one of Aja's maids, she retained her spot to try and catch anything else that slipped from the maid's lose tongue.

The King gave a signal and the music instantly stopped, the room fell silent,

"Kings, Queens, nobles and distinguished citizens of Nu Oarren, it is my joy to inform you all of a great blessing upon us, we have been waiting for such a day and this moment has come, your Empress Subira is to bare an heir to the throne, our first child"

the crowd erupted into applause, great cheers resonated around the room, the figure pushed through the crowd and threw off their mask roaring

"murderer you murderer!"

the unknown guest was brandishing a Saggittan knife, the assailant hurled it towards the King, a guard jumped in front of the dagger to protect the King and was killed instantly. Standing on their hind legs the alaka's roared, blocking the King and Empress as they were hastily escorted away.

Scattering in all directions the crowd screamed in fear for their own lives and were quickly pushed apart leaving a pathway for the protectors to swarm around the assailant, they unmasked the culprit, revealing a female Tau warrior, she struggled violently and in one swift motion using her speed, she swished her tail slapping the face of one protector, tripped up another and bit one of the guards on his forearm, before flying off into the crowd. In a tali she leapt into the rafters of the ballroom, amusing herself with their inflexibility. She danced from one rafter to another, laughing at the inability of the guards, she was too busy winding them up she missed her footing and tumbled to the ground in a heap, where the guards apprehended her using a force field net.

Pulling her down to the ground, one protector released another net over her and tightened it around her body, as they made the field more rigid the warrior screamed out at the top of her lungs

"murderers!"

The crowd hurled their fists franticly in the air and outbursts of anger exploded towards the Tau warrior engulfing the celebrations, the atmosphere was now filled with hatred.

They restrained her and escorted her away to the dark chambers, the Tau warrior shouted,

"your King is a murderer, he shall pay, and you will all pay for what was done!"

Tears fell from the warrior, her face riddled with pain. The guests all muttered amongst themselves wondering what this creature was talking about, wasn't it her tribe that King Javari had protected for many lucas? The mood was now dampened by this terrible ordeal; everyone was gradually evacuated from the ballroom, they all feared for Subira and the King.

One of the King's noble men called a protector and gave them a message to send to Javari. The guard flew off heading for the King's quarters. The nobleman then turned to the other two men and gave them a signal to leave the ballroom. The Tau woman kept screaming and repeating

"murderers, murderers!"

quickly disarming the force field net, one protector struck her over the head and knocked her out, the remaining four protectors lifted her off the ground and placed her on a restricting brace carrier and headed to the dark chambers for questioning.

King Javari entered the quarters from the tunnel along with his guards, at that moment the warriors knocked the door calling for chief Foruth. The door was opened, and the message was passed from the noble men.

Foruth closed the door and went to the King

"your highness the noblemen initiated the diversion but an intruder from the Tau tribe killed a guard, the dagger was to be delivered to you or the Empress, the guests have congregated in the courtyard and the upper royal gardens"

Javari slumped into a large chair, thinking about what just happened and if his wife Empress Subira would be safe,

"the Tau revenge begins" he muttered under his breath.

"Send word that both King and Empress are well, and the celebrations must continue" Murrock's tone sunk into rage

"I shall go and find out who this person is my King"

she was loyal to both Empress and Queen Adama and would not stop until she found out why this happened. King Javari nodded

"Then I shall go to the Queen your highness and give her Empress Subira's message.

"Find out what happened, how did this assailant get passed the protectors and the warlords?"

"Yes, your highness." Murrock left the quarters heading for the dark chambers.

The King looked at Foruth and Dacken with worry racing around in his thoughts, because they knew the truth.

***

The ashshun was falling fast, Aja had crossed most of the forest heading towards the Camu hills, her handmaids had now fallen asleep. The priestess removed her veil for a moment and stared at them toying with the idea of throwing them off the carriage for not staying awake. Noises within the forest broke her wicked thoughts. Her instincts tingled, she knew they were being followed, she urged her chauffeur to speed up, she scanned around the vessel until her eyes fell upon a weapon, carefully picking it up Aja covered her face back up then sat back staying alert for the rest of the journey.

***

Murrock arrived at the dark chambers full of rage, the dungeon walls displayed an array of torture devices, screens showed the prisoners in their cells. There were many cells positioned around the underground prison. The Tau woman was brought to a holding cell and propped up against the wall, her mouth had been gagged but you could still see and sense her deep-rooted revenge.

"Where is the assailant?" a guard pointed to a room door marked with the number 8,

"open the door!!" ordered Murrock.

As the door opened Murrock stared at the prisoner then took a small step back,

"what is it Murrock?" asked the guard.

Anger fell from her face

"nothing" she turned quickly towards the guards,

"Suspend all transmissions leave me with the prisoner."

The guards appeared puzzled with the order but left the cell and followed the captain's command. Murrock sheepishly shuffled towards the Tau woman, she recognized the markings but could not be sure, she stepped closer staring intensely, reading her with her eyes,

"Lani-ma?"

Murrock's tone was filled with disappointment, the Tau woman's expression altered, her eyes opened wide changing from rage to relief. Murrock pulled out the mouthpiece, the Tau woman coughed then gazed, moving her head and sniffing in the air,

"hmmmm Mmmrroccck."

Both Murrock and Lani-ma knew of each other, their paths crossed many lucas ago.

Lani-ma had saved Murrock's life and she swore to repay her back, the last time they saw each other was at Nu Jahri just before Murrock was given her post to guard the Empress,

"How? How could you do this? Are you mad? Are you stupid?"

Murrock slammed her hands against the restricting brace carrier

"my King, my Empress you will be put to death! You have gone insane!" she fumed.

"neveeeeeeeer, they will pay for my father's death, my mother hmmm Mmmurrrock, they killed thousands of my kin, your King yes, your King!" Lani-ma declared.

She began wriggling, trying her best to break free from the brace, she started shouting again.

"Be quiet Tau, my King! You speak blasphemy!" growled Murrock.

"Noooo! Murrrockkk, this is truth, ask your King why no one can cross my province, why there is no trade with my people, we have been isolated. They brought war. They lie, I tell you truth ask him, they lie, I will to die, if you do not seek the truth"

Lani-ma pleaded, her face did not show that she was lying and somehow Murrock knew she was telling the truth.

Murrock held onto both sides of Lani-ma's shoulders,

"if this is true, why have I not heard of this? Why didn't you find me and tell me Lani-ma? This does not make sense, wasn't it your King that declared war before?"

Lani-ma screamed from the pit of her stomach

"Nooooo! this is not true!" A suspicious guard hastily opened the cell door

"didn't I tell you to wait?" yelled Murrock, the door was quickly closed again.

"You must help Murroccckkkkkk, I will die on this day for I Lani-ma know this is truth," a deep but shallow breath spewed from her mouth

"but Murroccckkkkkk, you must do something for me."

The creature's voice softened, Murrock stepped back wondering how ridiculous and how dare Lani-ma ask for something in all of this. Her heart was beating fast, fear, anger, shame and grief all flew around her mind.

"This cannot be happening; I cannot free you Lani-ma!"
tears filled the creature's big brown eyes, her voice now with sadness

"not me, please, please..."
The door opened again but this time the guards walked in

"Murrock, chief Foruth, Dacken and the King are on their way."

"Murroccckkkk, please do this for me, our debt will be complete."
a guard answered abruptly

"are you in league with this animal? What does it mean? What will be complete? Are you a spy?"

Murrock swung her fist, punched the guard and he fell straight to the ground; gliding across the floor like it was filled with water, he ended up crashing into the cell wall.

"Do you defy me?"
She asked as the other guards helped him up to his feet, rubbing his jaw he glared at Murrock with

a vengeful eye, angry that this woman, even though she was a Captain warrior, had hit him to the floor, he walked embarrassed towards the cell door with the other guards who were now smirking over the blow. Lani-ma laughed

"huh, you've not changed my frienddddd."

The guards exchanged a look at each other, was the other guard, right? They stopped laughing and looked straight at Murrock.

"Stand outside and await for our King" she commanded.

Distrust raced in their minds and as the door closed to the cell one of the guards lent to the other

"we must report this to the Chief."

"Here take thissss Murroocckk, please, please in the middle"

Lani-ma looked up to her spiky hair, she then bent her head down revealing something attached to one of her clumped strands. Murrock yanked out a thin cylinder and looked suspiciously at it

"Is this a bomb?"

Lani-ma shook her head, Murrock reluctantly put it in her boot.

"Follow this, do this for me and I die in peace, I knew you would have been the one to come, to revenge your Empress and King, you are a loyal warrior my friend, I was told that you would come, she is never wrong, I thank you Murrock." Lani-ma breathed a sigh of relief.

"Who is never wrong? Who told you this? What is this you ask for me to follow?" she puzzled. Lani-ma was now quiet and didn't answer Murrock. A great sigh came from Murrock for she knew there was nothing she could do for her old friend she looked up to the ceiling to re-centre herself. Looking deep into Lani-ma's eyes she shrugged her shoulders to stand straight

"I will, without question,"

it was the first time that Murrock heard Lani-ma say her name without her native tongue, she knew now something was not right.

With her emotions threatening to overcome her composure, Murrock placed the gag back into Lani-ma's mouth, before it was fully fastened the Tau warrior spoke quietly

"this is for my kin, teach."

Still puzzled by what Lani-ma presented to her, Murrock wanted to pull the mouthpiece out. Her head quickly turned as she heard the door open Foruth and Dacken entered followed by the King, all three men fixed their eyes on Murrock, the warrior was bewildered but kept her stance.

"Leave Murrock and call for general Bakko to meet us here!"

Ordered the King, the three guards outside the cell followed Murrock as she walked passed, Foruth gazed back at Murrock, as one of the guards informed him of the suspicious conversation held with the assailant. As Murrock left the dark chambers, she felt uncertain of what Lani-ma said, she knew somehow Tau warriors would never lie, especially her friend. Murrock jumped on a flyer and left the chambers, heading towards the Queen's quarters.

Foruth smacked Lani-ma hard in her face

"is there more of you?"

"No Foruth let me speak with her, for it was my life she so desired, remove the gag." Javari ordered. Dacken wrenched the mouthpiece out, Lani-ma dropped her head and said nothing.

"This is your time to speak, so speak!"

Rage rose in King Javari, his fear seeping rapidly away, now instincts of protectiveness stepped in.

"You feel fear I smell it on you"
Lani-ma sniffed around at the guards and Javari.

"All of you, there is more of us and we will never stop until you all pay, I curse you, your Empress must die, you killed my Queen, my King, your Kingdom must fall!"

"How did you know how to pass all our checks? How?"
Dacken grabbed her by the throat and squeezed it tightly, choking her. Lani-ma cried out

"You have traitors in your mitts, you Jaaaaavarrrri made enemies that cannot be undone, it was easy to buy my way into this palace."
Dacken struck her again

"Who sold you plans? You beast, who?"
Lani-ma looked at the King and laughed, then started shaking her head and blinking her eyes quickly, in a fit like state.

"What's the matter with you?" Dacken struck her again.

The King turned away for a moment, he knew if he didn't silence her, the kingdom would turn against him, but if he kept her alive, she could be of some use.

"What did you converse to Murrock?"

"Who, that scum of the deepest pit, the same I said to you, you murderer!" she spat back at him.

"Gag her then take her to Calloway, I will get my answers."

Dacken struck her once more but this time knocked her out and forced the gag in her mouth. At this point Javari was sure she had witnessed the crime and was a casualty of war. Javari moved out of their way while they moved her out of the cell further down into the dark chambers.

Murrock flew grief stricken with sadness in her heart. The prophecy was unfolding but at what cost? Was she to lose everyone she had cared for? Did the King really sanction this genocide? It didn't make sense, how could this be hidden from her, was the story of the war declared by the Tau to be untrue? Who told Lani-ma that she would come? Why does her friend Lani-ma have to die?

What was this thing she had asked her to find? These feelings did not rest well with the warrior. As anger rose in her heart Murrock almost lost balance on the flyer, she regained herself and flew on towards the Queen's quarters.

---CHAPTER 8---

THE CAMU HILLS

Aja finally reached her destination, the atmosphere was magical, thousands of stars shone bright in the descending ashshun skies, fluorescent lights beamed outwardly from the hills and lit up the province. At the base of the hillside, huge settlements housed villagers from different tribes that claimed refuge from their former lands, many made a pilgrimage to become followers of the spiritual practise of Camu, this allowed them access into the hill, and they were given ceremonial duties. This land was classed as neutral, every tribe around Kemi knew not to bring any war against this place as they all lived in peace. Deep within the great mountains were internal rooms, to enter the mouth of the caverns that led to the sacred quarters, chief priests and priestesses had to travel through a vortex to gain access.

As Aja dismounted the carriage, she was greeted by two priests, one priest placed his hands on the three circles on her cheek and they mysteriously moved clockwise around her face, the other priest recited a mantra

"we move our body, our mind, our spirit, nature as one."

Then the two priests carried out the same ritual upon each other. Once the sequence was complete, their bodies became transparent and they escorted her to the middle cavern where the superiors waited. This was the only way to enter the hills to see the superiors, there were other routes accessible to followers, ordained trainees and rotating priests and priestess', but no one other than the high ordained could enter the sacred area of the superiors.

Strangely shaped figures moved around the translucent walls of the chambers of life, sat on seven large diamond thrones were the superiors. They were all dressed in white cloaks and each of them had the three circles on their cheeks, but their other facial features were not recognisable. The floor intermittently glistened and was covered with sacred symbols written by the Aluke tribe and the pure ones. Aja took her place in the centre of the floor

"Superiors" the priestess knelt before them bowing her head. They spoke simultaneously

"There lies a disturbance Daktari, speak of the sighting."

The priestess held her staff and began the sighting as she spoke, around the walls, imprints of what she saw became clearer to the superiors, images of King Javari appeared amongst other figures.

"Cease!"

they raised their right hands pointing to Aja, her eyes instantly returned to green.

"The prophecy begins, but you know this Daktari you know of the seed to shift"

"Mala obl gacheru, your sightings are impure you can no longer be Subira's high priestess, this will be written."

"What?!"

Aja scrambled to her feet clutching her chest as she screamed

"my heart? Yes, filled with poison from loss, you all feel that I am bitter hearted and even a spy? Never, I tell you this, there was something else within the quarters, I have been the finest seer you have ever seen and ever trained, I came for answers, how can you all deny me this?!"

Her eyes widened and her veins throbbed, the priestess spun around the room staring at the seven superiors.

"Aja be still, we cannot grant you this, you say you are the supreme, then tell us why you could not see the sighting, you were not ready to leave us at Camu, you were not, what have you done Aja? There is unbalance, what is hidden shall become clear."

The priestess dropped her staff and ripped the veil from her face.

"Then tell me what it means, tell me, I...I could die if I do not interpret my sighting, why is this? Why...is... this?" Aja pleaded for an answer.

Each of the superiors disappeared leaving Aja standing alone, a faint voice resonated

"it is written."

The priestess dropped to her knees, enraged and upset, the superiors reappeared at the upper temple where their physical beings were sitting; the appearance in the room with Aja was an imprint of themselves.

"We must summon the guardians from the fold of Aluke, Aja Daktari must be contained, what is revealed shall change our universe, she has gained a block, even our eyes cannot see, but the King is her connection."

The superiors agreed. Aja fled the cavern they had now confirmed the seed of Javari, Subira must be pregnant, her pain grew and now she knew what she had to do.

--- CHAPTER 9 ---

THE WATER ISLANDS

A group of protectors had flown ahead of the convoy; checking the region, gently rubbing her round pregnant stomach the Empress peered out of the window longing for her husband. The carriage was cloaked, the naked eye could not see or hear it as it moved above the sea, as it soared towards the Island, the only thing visible was the rippling foaming water leaving a trail. Murrock sat haunted by the bellowing of the execution horn, they had heard while leaving the palace, announcing Lani-ma's death. At some point she had to leave the Empress to find out what the Tau warrior had left for her. Although loyal to the royal family Murrock was disheartened, her one true friend from since she had left her land was now dead for attempting murder. Both Murrock and Empress Subira sat in their own anguish bound for an unknown path.

Nu Jahri was known as the water islands and lay south of Nu Oarren, the terrain stood high upon layers of green grass mounds. At times the royal family used the water islands as a relaxation retreat. It was once said that the islands had floated around for many lucas until one day it just stopped in the darkness of ashshun under the formation of the lari stars, the natives then built foundation blocks to prevent the island from floating away. The dense bundled hottonia plant that coated the belly of the land masses, created the miraculous buoyancy no other island possessed.

The land was almost impenetrable, a gauzy sparkling water shield surrounded the skies and the sacred sea creatures the ulowpillors had protected the sea and the lands over hundreds of lucas, they migrated together as the island journeyed. These gigantic ancient eels swam beautifully within the waters, their scales shimmered generating magical melodies, with colours of gold, orange and green their sight was spectacular to behold, at the ashshun they illuminated the seas with their bellowing but beautiful sounds that spread across the island answering each other in a playful way.

The waters had great healing powers which served well for the farming communities, many of their crops were exported around the planet, the Tau province and Nu Jahri were the only two places that could grow the wonda plants because of their wet and rich soil. The overseer of the land was Gogo Amakia; it was said that she was over two hundred lucas old. Blessed with great knowledge and wisdom of Ramla the ancient arts of predicting the future, Gogo, along with her elders had the ability to provide protection for the pregnant Empress.

Along with her servants Gogo waited on the bridge at the sea front for the arrival of the Empress' party. The protectors positioned themselves at the opening of the water gates, once the carriage flew through, they surrounded the vessel until they landed safely. As they entered the gates, the cloaking system of the craft faded because of the flowing water defence wall. The carriage manoeuvred around the docking bay near to Gogo's thatched hut. The inhabitants of the water island observed the craft moving across their skies. Everything within Nu Jahri's settlement was made of natural hemp materials.

Clusters of spectacular green land masses stretched as far as the eye could see. Surrounding the waterfront, were groups of magnificent prehistoric trees that wrapped around the buildings creating organic monuments, the undergrowth was filled with gigantic colourful keba flowers and scattered around the settlement were exotic fruit trees.

The thick woven hemp ropes that draped to form the bulky bridges linked everything together. Deep beneath the islands descending to the sea floor were huge wooden structures that stabilised the island, tall bamboo trees spiralled around the moss-covered rocks. Grand gazeboes decorated the surrounding areas, which gave shelter to the natives from the tropical climate of Nu Jahri. Enormous land creatures moved around the islands gracefully, their large blue mains drifted against the tropical breeze.

At the edge of the bridge toddled Gogo, full of uncountable wisdom, she bared a warm motherly smile upon her wrinkled brown face. Her head was wrapped in a yellow cloth that spanned outwards like a blossoming flower, the hem of her brown robe was covered with traditional symbolic patterns. Around her neck hung a huge beaded necklace worn by all the elders and fastened to the top of a wooden staff in her left hand crowned was a rose quartz stone.

As the party emerged from the carriage,

Gogo motioned for Murrock to come,

"leave tonight Murrock,"

she whispered in her ear while embracing her with a hug

"Subira will be safe."

Murrock looked puzzled for a moment, then recalled how powerful the old woman was and connected to what Lani-ma had said. Gogo instructed the group into the hut.

"Come eat, protectors you too, come Empress, sit please sit, all will be well."

The old woman could sense both Murrock and the Empress' pain and danced them into the hut.

The giggling voice of the old woman brought calm to everyone as she swung her large hips ushering them eat, her servants carried in trays of freshly cooked fish, bread, fruits and refreshments, in the corner of the hut sat musicians who were playing music from the kori instrument and Gep deep skinned drums, which soothed the spirit of the party.

"Here is where you will rest Empress" motioning to a door.

"Come, eat, your strength is even more important now."

Gogo continued to dance around clapping her hands and shaking her bottom, she smiled humming along to the music, her heart was filled with delight for she knew who was in her presence and consciously changed the energy of everyone.

Gogo raised her cup

"long live King Javari, Empress Subira and the heir to the throne."

The group stood up saluting the royal family. Subira smiled and nodded sheepishly, her thoughts were still with her husband, she began to nibble at the sweet juicy fruits, as they melted in her mouth, it triggered a childhood memory that brought a calmness and warmth over her making her feel a little bit more settled. Some of the elders moved from their seats and kept the party entertained with their traditional moves and cheerful laughter; swishing their flowing white skirts, even the protectors and guards cheered them on and were soon dragged in to dance with the old women. The Empress now more joyful, clapped away with giggles as the old women spun her guards' round and round. Even Murrock embraced the atmosphere and secretly shook her large shoulders to the music. After the meal was finished and the other elders had retired to their huts, Gogo and Subira took a stroll out to the balcony.

"It is so beautiful here, the school of ulowpillors are just magnificent, they make the waters seem so peaceful." marvelled Subira.

The creatures moved up and down riding the waters, they disappeared then reappeared further down the sea.

"Empress, still waters run deep, they make it look calm that is true, in the water hides many stories, other universes, as above and as down below." Gogo mused.

Gogo's eyebrows lifted as she peered down at Subira's right hand spotting the leckon bracelet, "Empress, who gave you this?"

"Oh, this bracelet, my mother Queen Adama gave it to me, I was told not to take it off."

"Hmmmm" murmured the old woman she looked out to the waters then gazed up into the skies,

"no, do not. This must not be taken off until you give birth, it must also be kept safe like you." Subira nodded at Gogo and looked back out to the waters in silence, without questioning Gogo why.

"My Empress you must soon rest, you must be exhausted." Subira took a short but quiet breath

"May I have a moment alone Gogo?"

"Yes, your highness."

The old woman bowed then walked back into the hut, two protectors got up and stood near the door to the balcony. Gogo beckoned Murrock to her room

"Shut the door and sit."

Murrock sat on the little wooden stool, trying desperately not to fall off it, she noticed the animals roaming around in the room

"they will not harm you Murrock" laughed the old woman.

"You must leave, for your journey has just begun, let me see"
she gestured with her hand towards the warrior's boots, Murrock instantly knew she was referring to the small cylinder that Lani-ma gave her.

"How did you know Gogo?" she questioned, amused.

"I know much and say little, hmm she was here not long ago." She unfolded the cylinder, which held a piece of paper, it displayed a map, the name Nyper was written at the location. Murrock hesitated for a moment

"You knew of the plot against the King and Empress?"

"Hmmm, Nyper interesting" she began giggling.

"No not at all, now that, that was surprising to me too my warrior, I did know what ever she was up to that you would somehow be there."

Murrock looked at her even more puzzled, trying her best to figure out how she knew this would happen and not seeing this side of Lani-ma. "We all have many sides Murrock, come see my map." Lying on shelves were scrolls, she ran her hand from left to right mumbling to herself until she found what she was looking for.

"When you return bring some ban roots and seavan spices, oh they make a great tea, here" she pointed to the map and instructed Murrock on how to get there.

"Take this too"
Gogo handed her a big furry bag and put the map inside, from her closet she drew out a hooded cloak and handed it to Murrock.

"You must wear this, camouflage your armour, you will return back to Bernal one day, when the Solomon child is ready, and the prophecy's beginning is there"

"how do you know this Gogo?" questioned Murrock.

"It's in the scrolls Murrock"
Gogo giggled through her words, then stopped abruptly staring at the warrior

"I, I am heartbroken too my warrior, she was such a big hearted prankster"
tottering over to Murrock she gave her a big hug around her waist, the warrior felt awkward but patted her on her little shoulders while resisting the tears threatening to fall. With her wrinkled fingers, Gogo pointed back to the shelf

"ancient that is true, but believe it or not, it will all come to pass."
Murrock side eyed her

"when will I know it is time to return?"

"you will know when, someone is guarding it for me, you will know, now come, come!" They walked out the room into the main area,

"Murrock is to get me some ban roots and spices, she is to go to Bernal, the trading village, I have need of them." The guards nodded

"Do you wish us to accompany you Captain? You can take my flyer" handing Murrock his helmet

"I think it will fit"
the guard mocked the female warrior's large head. Murrock frowned and walked off to the dock walking into the cheeky guard toppling him to the ground. Gogo chuckled as she remembered both

Lani-ma and Murrock fighting for power, this bullying display was so natural to them both.

"Be back before the rising of the suns, my warrior" Murrock nodded.

"Our Empress will be safe" Gogo could feel the delay in her steps and Murrock could sense that she could, leaving with a smile she headed for the flyer.

Subira entered the room with a surprised look

"where is my captain warrior Murrock going?"

"On an errand for me Empress, she will be back soon."

"Murrock goes alone?"

"Yes, yes, she knows these lands, it will not take her long and besides my Empress are you not tired now?" Subira gestured in agreement

"I do require rest Gogo" the old woman could see that the Empress was putting on a brave face.

"Come Your Highness" with a gentle bow Gogo moved, guiding Subira to her quarters.

"Before I depart, can a message be sent to inform the King that we are safe, it must be long enough now and safe to make contact."

One of the protectors nodded, took the brooch from the Empress and left the hut,

"I shall bid you all a good ashshun."

The Empress was unaware of the attack by the Tau woman and who was at large waiting to intercept any communications. The Empress' ladies in waiting accompanied her to her room. Gogo guided the other protectors and guards to their quarters, leaving four guards stationed outside the Empress' door. The other protector walked across the bridge guided by a servant to send the message to the King.

--- CHAPTER 10 ---

THE LARI STARS

Now all the guests had left the palace, the servants swiftly cleared up all mess of the celebrational steamers and rubbish that was left scattered around the ballroom, although the entertainment had continued throughout the evening into the late ashshun, Javari spent a duration of time in his quarters, but made a short appearance to reassure his guests that all was well and being handled, he announced to the crowd that the Empress was resting and sent her blessings to them all. When greeting his family members, he had no desire to speak to them but acted nobly repelling any questions by switching subjects, in his mind this wasn't the occasion for him to celebrate but to unmask plots against him and his immediate family. The royal army were busy checking the grounds for devices and any other suspicious indicators.

All the guests were scanned again as they left, the protection fence was now up by the main entrance. More protectors were brought to the palace including the warlords who are not often seen. Nothing or no one was to get in or out without the King's permission or knowledge.

"This is a good time, send for the guardians."

Javari instructed Dacken and Foruth

"Yes your highness."

They responded and sent the other guards to summon the guardians at the cave of the sacred mount near the palace grounds.

The noblemen were busy as one began plotting the lari stars he said,

"Yes your Highness, they move into a new position, it has begun." Javari walked towards the balcony

"May I see?" the nobleman handed the King his telescope and he looked up in the ashshun skies to see the start of the realignment.

The lari constellation and nine planets were slowly merging to create a gateway to a powerful cosmic energy that they hoped would bring back balance to their solar system, this super event could change the face of their dying Kemi. Every fifty lucas it was written that a child or several would carry the key to unlocking the hiding places of the scrolls that contained the power, in the wrong hands it could be used as a lethal weapon. Many tribes fought for this holy anointing, using false scrolls and myths they tried to bring forth the complete prophecy but failed and the planet suffered from their ordeals. Over two hundred lucas Kemi drew intense energy from the lari star's unbalanced alignment, it was written that two energies descended upon the planet and these frequencies brought about a tremendous disruption. If the prophecy could not be fulfilled in their generation, it was feared the disruption could bring about complete annihilation of their solar system. The Solomon royal family may be the final chance to shift the balance and save the planet or evacuation would be their only other hope to survive.

The King gazed across the skies and saw five shooting stars moving south north. He stared intently at the moving objects, something seemed strange in their formation, it seemed too precise, he immediately beckoned one of the noblemen to see for themselves. As the nobleman scoured the ashshun skies he could only glimpse the trail left by the objects. The nobleman quickly beckoned a guard to send a message to the flyers to patrol the skies, Javari glanced at him, knowing that what was told to him by Queen mother Adama was now so very true.

Just before the royal wedding, Adama reluctantly shared with Javari who was now thirty lucas, of the battle at the fold of Aluke. Both she and her husband had witnessed the event, the stories which were re-counted over many lucas were not myths but truth. Adama presented Javari the leckon bracelet, revealing more truth to what had happened and the part she now played. It was never spoken to the Empress, as giving her this information could change her and affect the future of their planet. The King searched the stars knowing that this was a historical moment, something fated, he walked back to his chair and asked everyone to leave for a moment. Guards and noblemen left the quarters, Dacken and Foruth stayed alert, waiting outside the door until they were summoned again. As Javari shifted in his chair to face the window he pulled for his skinny wooden pipe, replaying the words of Adama round and round in is mind. Once again, he remembered his father's last words to him before he went to war, he had to live this out and he had to see this to the end. As the smoke drifted into the air, he stretched himself out in attempt to release all the tension in his shoulders and body. Feeling his heartbeat and breath steadying itself he gently closed his eyes to meditate, just for a moment he needed stillness, just for a moment.

--- CHAPTER 11---

THE TRADING VILLAGE

Murrock sped through the desert wiping the sweat from her brow from the ashshuns heat. The warrior flew through the Kiya boarders, she took rest for a while to quench her thirst and filled up her container for the rest of the journey. It wasn't long before she arrived at the village, ahead of her stood the towering brass gates of the trading village, moving closer beautiful blue flamed torches lit with the natural oils from the village's ground springs, guided the warrior to Bernal. The street's sand became blood red from the heated underground pools, even at ashshun the dusty streets were full of activity, it was a thriving economy, traders interacted here from many provinces and other planets near Kemi.

The boulevard was packed with a blanket of colourful fruit peddlers, sellers of fine cloth and wonderful shades of dyes for fabrics. Dancing drumming women, jugglers, fire breathers, zodiac magicians, spiritual interpreters and even gangs of street children were riding on the backs of the wild desert cats that surrounded the streets. The sweet smell of colourful spices, incense and herbs filled the warm ashshun air, the combination of the different dialects buzzed around the village like melodies. Murrock scuttled along in and out of the jigsawed sand buildings and congested streets, dodging the people that stepped out of nowhere. No one was suspicious of the warrior on the royal flyer wearing a helmet, for the natives were notorious for steeling and trading anything within the village. The warrior flew around the roads following the map, it was not long before she arrived at the location of the street's plaza given by Gogo.

The itchy rope irritated her and made her fidget, which almost made Murrock drive into a kianda food hut. She asked the vendors for the whereabouts of the hut, they pointed in the direction of a building to the left then quickly closed the food hatch door. The warrior slowed down dismounting the flyer she studied the door fronts, a soft voice called over to her

"come, I have been expecting you."

Under a porch lay slumped a fat figure dressed in a red and green hooded robe. As Murrock approached the figure she saw it was a Tau man puffing on a keba powder pipe.

"I, mm Hajj"

the man looked up and down the warrior's body

"I am Murrock, you know why I'm here?"

"Yes indeeeeed" he replied.

The man's face changed for a moment

"hmmm," he hesitated "so, so she is dead?"

Murrock sighed

"It is so, she was my friend."

Hajj patted the warrior's arm as to pay respect to her.

"Did you know of her intentions?" asked Murrock.

Hajj sniggered

"There was something that troubled her, but all I knew for sure was that, she said her friend would come for..."

Murrock quickly interrupted Hajj to shadow the emotions rising up in her

"So where is this item I must collect?"

"item!!"

a bellowing hoot danced into the ashshuns air

"it's more than an item, I'm glad you came for her,"

the warrior side eyed Hajj

"for her?"

Murrock froze in shock,

"a child?"

"Yes, I would have sold her, I have no time raising a..."

his words were drowned by a screaming child.

"She is in there; you will need this" the man handed Murrock some sticks of ban root.

"What is in there?"

Murrock stood now disturbed, she wasn't trained for this. No combat tactics would prepare her for this new post.

"Hmm, Lani-ma's daughter"

the man laughed and continued smoking on his pipe. Murrock took the ban roots and cautiously entered the room. Lani-ma! my Lani-ma has a daughter, with, who? She peered around the quarters, a screaming cackling shriek penetrated the warrior's ears, she tried to block it out 9 sticking her gloved fingers in her ears, she scanned the room but could not locate the child.

"She is a fast one I tell you; she is going to be quicker than Lani-ma and her..."

"arghhhh"

Murrock felt a bite on her thigh.

"Yes, she bites" the fat man giggled.

"Better you than me."

Murrock pulled the wriggling child from her leg, the moment she smelt the ban roots the child wrapped herself around Murrock's arm and bit a piece of the stick.

The child was chewing away then peeping up at the warrior's face. Murrock saw Lani-ma's eye's which brought a small smile.

"What is the meaning of Nyper? Murrock attempted to gently stroke her spikey hair

"That's her name, Nyper, she looks odd for a Tau tribe don't you think? I think she is mixed with...."

Hajj was just about to finish when, the child's ears pricked up, then chaos, she started franticly running around Murrock's body biting and scratching at her with alarming speed, tearing into her robe.

"Put some ban roots in the bag" Hajj ordered

"what?!"

Nyper jumped off Murrock, sending the clay pots and pans clanging around the room. Murrock got hit in the head twice but was able to dodge the other missiles, finally she put all of the ban roots in the bag

"ahhhh, I wouldn't do that if I was you" shouted Hajj,

"I'll deal with this my way, old man."

Murrock rubbed her hands and started calling Nyper.

The child continued jumping around using Murrock as target practise. The warrior rubbed her head and ducked left and right from the pots been thrown, she attempted to speak like Lani-ma "hmmm Nypeeeerr."

The eyes of the child opened wide and her ears pricked up again, she slowly started moving towards Murrock, then threw another pot at her, as she repeated her name again and again the child moved closer until she pounced on her shoulder.

Nyper started to rub her head against Murrock's helmet, the aroma of the ban roots struck her nose and lured her to jump into the big furry bag and continue munching.

"hmm, she is receptive to this"

Murrock mused, while she adjusted her shredded robe, she felt in control again and showed Hajj that she was now successful.

"You will see warrior, here"

shaking his head with laugher, he then handed Murrock a large bag of ban roots; she fastened them to the flyer and secured the bag with Nyper inside chewing away, then bid Hajj farewell and headed to buy the spices for Gogo before flying back to Nu Jahri before dawn.

--- CHAPTER 12 ---

THE GUARDIANS

The priests searched the grounds for Aja, but she was far away when the guardians of Aluke arrived at the upper temple. They could transport themselves using the symbols around the chambers and special landmarks. A shivering breeze spiralled into the room. Gradually figures began to appear one after another until the guardian's human forms became visible, there now stood eight cloaked guardians four men and four women. Above each of their heads shone an orb of light, each one flickered a different colour. These orbs gave them the abilities to speak any language within Kemi and other galaxies.

One of the male guardians advanced, followed closely by the group, he took the hood from his head and looked at all of the priests and priestesses,

"Daktari knows more than you see"

Wallak who was one of the priestesses spoke,

"we felt the presence of darkness, this is why we summoned you, Daktari's full movements could not be seen, she knows much more now, we cannot stop what is to unfold, for it is written..."

"what of our kin?" questioned one of the priestesses.

The guardian stepped back

"prepare to leave Camu hills in four camalas from the awakening dawn, one hibb before the new light, for it will begin, the realignment. We will guide you to new-born lands, call for us no more until then."

All the guardians stepped back and disappeared from view. The priests and priestesses sat down quietly, closing their eyes and bowing their heads, the symbols on the floor began spinning around making a powerful ringing sound, then just like the guardians they disappeared. The priests and priestesses gazed at each other, knowing that the prophecy was so very true. As they looked at their hands, they could no longer move freely and fluidly as before, as they realised their powers were starting to diminish; the prophecy was starting to unfold.

They would become powerless, once the prophecy unfolds, they would be normalised, they gazed at each other for a few moments, breaking the silence one of the priests turned to the other six

"how can this be stopped? This is our life; we were born with our gifts and now to lose them?"

Wallak raised her hand with the power that she had left, picked him up in the air and pushed him into a pillar of the temple,

"speak not of this again, this is our destiny! It is written, do not make the rivers of ego echo and poison your spirit brother! Our time is endless, our souls are oceans, leave us, for the bitterness of Aja creeps within you like a vicious creature, meditate."

As he stumbled to the floor, he scampered over to Wallak, bowed his head and kissed her hand

"Wallak, pray I was filled with conditions of human flesh, forgive me, our shift begins." He turned away then disappeared down the spiral stairs from the upper temple to search for Aja.

Way above in the skies, a flock of Saggittans flew bound to their home of Saggitta.

Aja looked up, watching them disappear into the ashshun heavens, her carriage was headed back to Nu Oarren. Focused on her next move, she knew things were about to change and she could not stay within the palace walls for much longer, she planned to leave Nu Oarren and had made arrangements for somewhere to go in a few camalas but had not anticipated on leaving so soon. She muttered under her breath with a vengeful tongue

"You will feel my pain Subira."

Her maids sat up right for Aja gave them a scolding for falling asleep, although their eyes were blood shot red, they fought back the tiredness as they dared not to even take a slight nap. Aja's thoughts were on Javari, she knew in her blackened heart they knew of her husband's death. The priestess was unable to use the power of future sighting on anyone except Empress Subira, they were bonded, and this could not be undone except by death. Aja bent down and took from her bag a medal that belonged to her beloved imperial Officer Duke. Holding it close to her chest, the heart of the priestess had a moment of warmth and remembrance of love, seeing her husband receiving his honorary award for his dedication to the royal army. Carefully she pulled from her pocket a small box, she gently opened it up to look inside but closed it quickly from the rushing wind. Somehow, she knew the King had the key to the truth and this ashshun she would extract it from him and Empress Subira was going to pay for her pain.

***

King Javari had received the message from his guards that the guardians would return to the sacred mount near the palace at sunrise, they also sent a warning for the King to capture Aja once she returned to the palace. Javari was also asked a strange request by the guardians; he must be moved before sun set to another room and no water should be in the quarters with him. Javari gave instructions to Dacken and two guards to prepare a room for him. The patrols flyer docks were stationed at every perimeter and outside the priestess' chambers, guards were armed and ready for her arrival, even the warlords were summoned, many of them scattered around the outside wall of the palace and within the Nu Oarren City. The citizens watched as they marched around the streets, they had heard of the attack on the royal family and even became suspicious of their Tau friends. A force field surrounded the inner walls although it was set at lower voltage, anything too high could cause harm to the province and affect the tectonic plates, which were already fragile. One of Aja's maids knew of the secret entrance where she could not be detected, holding a flame torch, wrapped warmly in a long green velvet cape she waited patiently in the shimmering cold tunnel for the priestess to return.

--- CHAPTER 13 ---

THE BONDING OF MURROCK AND NYPER

As Murrock flew towards Nu Jahri, a pungent stench drifted upwards to hit the warrior in her nostrils.

"For the love of my ancestors what is that?" she spat, disgusted.

The scent made her gag overwhelming her with nausea.

"uh owww, heee ahhh"

came the laughter of Nyper along with a growling stomach from the bag, Murrock now understood what the fat man Hajj was warning her about, the creature must have eaten too many ban roots. The smell was too much so she slowed down and dismounted the flyer, as soon as she unlocked the bag she saw Nyper's face straining in pain, another wave of potent stench exploded from the bag, Murrock was hit in the face with what brewed within the furry bag. Nyper jumped out throwing the soiled, wet and clumped contents all over Murrock, she yelled in disgust and dropped the bag of ban roots.

"You disgusting animal, Nyperrrrr you threw your poop? Your stinky poop?" Murrock shouted at the top of her voice

"ahhhhhhh"

flicking off the mess as quickly as she could.

Nyper jumped around and shook her bottom in the air towards Murrock and gave off a mighty noise that bellowed into the ashshuns air, she then ran off into the darkness, laughing at her new stepmother covered in her waste matter.

"Ahhhhhhhhhh you will pay, ahhh Nyperrrrrrrrrrr"

Murrock yelled once again and chased the child into the trees and bushes. The warrior searched around trying to find the child while she continued to brush off the poop covering her. Murrock picked up a stick and started poking the bushes to disturb Nyper. She also hit her chest plate to create light that beamed into the bushes creating shadows of the child darting to and fro between the thick bushes.

There was a small oasis pool on the other side of the bushes, Murrock peeled off the repulsive soiled robe and washed herself frantically in horror of the ordeal. As she cleaned her helmet and bag from debris, she separated the edible ban roots from those soiled by the poop, giggling Nyper appeared from the bush.

"Why did you do this?! Child, this is not correct!"

Murrock stared at Nyper who was now flipping around the grass holding her stomach, still laughing and repeating Murrock

"hmm, not ccccorrect."

Murrock shouted at the top of her lungs

"Nyppperrrrr, Lani-ma would be not pleased, not pleased at all!"

"Lani mar"

Nyper called back, her laughter stopped, and her eyes slowly opened

"marrrr."

The child's face drooped with sadness; the corners of her mouth turned downwards.

"marrrr!"

Nyper's eyes welled and she scurried towards Murrock. The trauma of the missile attack soon faded from the warrior, as she saw the posture of the child's slump, her eyes now full of broken-hearted tears, the youngster started crawling towards the warrior and cried. Nyper climbed into the arms of Murrock, the warrior slowly stroked her head, Nyper glanced around almost waiting for the arrival of her mother.

"Be well Nyppperrrrr, I will look after you." Murrock wiped the tears from her sorrowful eyes, then sat in silence. A weighty sadness and humbleness overcame her as she continued stroking Nyper's head, she was now open to accept her new responsibility. Lani-ma would have wanted this, she wouldn't have trusted anyone else to take on this role.

The glistening stars began to fade as the bosom of dawn rose, the ashshun birds flew in murmuration giving them a taste of something spectacular as the yante opened. Nyper's eyes opened wide at the sight and kept closing as she fought back her sleep, it was a beautiful moment, one which the warrior did not experience often. Murrock was one of the strongest members of her clan and was now humbled with the honour of raising Lani-ma's child. As the child fell asleep the warrior whispered over her

"I will tell you one day of a great warrior that saved my life, she was my friend, your mother Lani-ma."

Murrock flagged away the water from the bag, tore some of her robe and used it to swaddle the child for comfort. The warrior spent a moment looking into the pastel purple and orange sky knowing that her life purpose was unfolding again.

***

Dawn was on the horizon as the carriage approached the border of Nu Oarren where they could see an assembly of guards. Aja gave a signal to her chauffeur and he veered away from the boundary line. The carriage flew unseen and glided along the river's edge, stopping in the forest by the mouth of the waters, parallel to the south gate. Aja stepped out of the carriage and turned to the chauffeur, he got out holding a weapon to join Aja, he then programmed the carriage to move further down the river, initiating the cloaking system to hide from the guards patrolling the Nu Oarren boarders.

As the carriage began to disappear, the priestess started to chant the ancient words to open the secret underwater stairway, she signalled to the chauffeur that he needed to dispose of the maids. The maids saw this exchange and started to tremble, two short shots and it was over, both maids fell to the ground. The chauffeur dropped the weapon beside them, both Aja and her chauffeur walked towards the water. As Aja stepped into the water an opening appeared, revealing a dripping stairwell, they both continued down, leaving the dead maids near the water's edge along with the weapon. As they disappeared under the river, the entrance closed again, hiding the secret doorway to the underground tunnels.

--- CHAPTER 14 ---

SAGGITTA AND VOLKER

High up in the icy coated mountains of Saggitta, east of Nu Oarren, the two clan families assembled to thrash out the ongoing disagreement that had been brewing for eighteen lucas since the second war occurred. Messages were sent back and forth between both tribes until the day came when they decided to meet, this was spurred by the attack on the Solomon family. A peace treaty was signed by all kingdoms in Kemi; King Javari who was fourteen lucas along with Skylan the King of Saggitta, Walker the King of the Volker clan, the Kiandans, the Tau and Gep tribes. Land was given to the guardians and they spent their lives at the fold of Aluke to help protect the planet. After the attack on the Solomon family all eyes were on Skylan and the Saggittans. It had reached boiling point and another war could threaten all provinces again.

The atmosphere between both tribes was tense, the King of Saggitta stood at his balcony overlooking the mountain tops, their large based bodies hidden by the misty clouds drifting across his province. He turned back to join the warriors who were arguing amongst themselves, the weaponry store of the Saggittans had been raided some time ago, after being closed for eighteen lucas and word had been spread that the Volker clan were behind it. He remembered how when he was at the age of eighteen. Young and stupid, power hungry and stubborn, though his sheer greed driven ambition could have caused the destruction of so many. As he listened to the arguments being tossed around like leaves in the wind, he stared at Prince Kaydor's flaming mouth and was angry that he saw his old childish self in him, a burning sensation roared out of his stomach and cut the air,

"enough!"

Skylan marched up to the brawling group of warriors and royals who stood ready to battle.

"So, you feel fit to blame my kin, my people?" the aggravated Prince Kaydor of Volker rose and steamed across the room to rest beside his father King Walker.

The Volker people are known as the earthly kin as they are able to harness solar energy and use it as a weapon for good or evil. Their two-toned hair of ginger and blonde separated them from other tribes, their skin would radiate whenever they conjured up their powers, like the Saggittan clan, their abilities shifted after the first war when Skylan invaded the fold of Aluke. They were feared by so many people, their tribe were known as an arrogant breed as they saw themselves as superior beings, their lands were filled with gold which made it a wealthy country but could never match the multitude of gold deposits in the Anobi mines. The Saggittan people had a remarkable ability to bare the cold, but this would strain their resources to fly. They were able to harness the sun's rays and transform it into energy that allowed them to fly for long periods of time, villagers named them Malaikas. Over many lucas the Saggittans mastered skills of manipulating air, rumours festered that King Skylan had stolen some power from the fold of Aluke which gave his tribe greater abilities. No one had proof but evidence was there when Skylan was happy to make their Saggittan strike weapons obsolete after the last war and amnesty was soon in place which led to Skylan signing the treaty. King Walker stood almost face to face with King Skylan, their eyes were piercing each other's souls. Their breath pumping from their mouths into the cold; forming tiny pockets of clouds.

"I tell you this, after the attack upon King Javari and the Empress there is foul play at hand, who broke into our weaponry and used our knife? Why would we do this to our own and destroy peace, we have not used weapons for over eighteen lucas!"

Skylan rose a few inches from the ground stretching beams of light out in fury.

The Volker Prince Kaydor glared through the light which provoked Skylan even more

"We were there, we saw what you saw, it was a Tau warrior woman that's true, she was brandishing one of your knives! Their tribe are swift enough and can endure the cold conditions like you, did you open the doors and turn your eyes? They can climb the snowy peaks of your mountains, was your power draining from your city's stolen resources? Are you being angry because you sided with Javari and could steal no more?!"

Even his own father shivered at his son's words, he was waiting for a definitive attack from Skylan. Mura the first-born daughter of Skylan drew her fists together and sucked in the air, in one swoop she punched and missed Kaydor in the face, she swung so hard that she spun around and fell on the floor puffing and panting from the exertion. Her guards jumped to her attention and pulled her to her feet, awaiting a signal from their King. Walker's hands started to glow, from both tribes a jeering tension swirled around the room. No one was focusing on a solution, the spirit of joy for a battle was now taking shape. Skylan was hovering in the air wavering with anger and toying with the thought that it wasn't logical, it just did not make sense at all.

"Quieten your boy Walker!"

he finally said, Kaydor stepped back to prepare his strike, when suddenly splinters of wood fell from the rafters, everyone looked up in shock. The youngest son of King Skylan, Ulen had listened quietly until he could take no more, he flew up into the rafters and blasting them to shake loose some more wood to disperse the negative energy. Once everyone's attention was taken off their egos he shouted

"stop, stop, stop fighting something is not right, can't you see this? A Tau warrior went to kill the King, their species are not warmongers, my father told me the stories and tales that their tribe were attacked by King Javari's men. I believe this to be so, we need to know the truth and who stole from my father!" while floating down to rest on his father shoulders until his father floated down to the floor.

Silence descended upon the room, everyone stood humbled and in agreement of the little boy. Skylan looked up at his son, slowly lifting him off his shoulders, he felt extremely proud of his little prince's bravery.

"He is right!"

Kaydor walked shamefully towards the prince, he bowed smiling at him,

"Your father should be proud of such a fine and noble son with great wisdom and you are only five lucas?"

Kaydor slowly turned to peer at Mura

"this makes a change" Skylan grunted at Kaydor,

his son bowed back at the prince then flew up again but perched on his sister's shoulder, they both exchanged a mischievous smile then stared straight at Prince Kaydor. Skylan strolled over to his children, grabbed their heads shaking them lovingly and kissed them both on their foreheads, the children returned the gesture by playfully kissing his cheeks at the same time. Although it was a cold room, an infectious warmth of love brought a positive resonance to everyone. King Walker glanced at his son, trying to remember the last time he had hugged or kissed him, he could not find a memory. Prince Kaydor took a deep breath

"We heard tales of a dark soul from Nu Oarren, an outcast, it is said he is in alliance with Commander Grave and the assassin's clan, your son is right. Instead of fighting amongst ourselves we must find out what is being planned, I, I will send out my squadron to investigate."

Walker stepped up to Skylan and reached out his right hand, Skylan stared for a minute then shook his hand firmly excepting a truce

"I too will deploy some of my ground soldiers, together we will find out what is being schemed."

Both men declared an allegiance and continued their debate as comrades on who would plot against the treaty.

--- CHAPTER 15 ---

THE REVENGE OF AJA

It wasn't long before Aja met her faithful maid in the tunnel, she explained to the priestess what she had overheard and what had taken place at the banquet. Aja became angry

"This means she is no longer here, she was not at the banquet, hmm... they must have sent her away" the maid look puzzled with what Aja said,

"High Priestess forgive me, but how could she not be there?"

"What you saw was an imprint, it was the nobles doing, let us go to my chambers, I must collect my scrolls."

"An imprint?"

The baffled maid scurried behind the chauffeur pestering him to find out if he knew what Aja meant. The secret tunnel led them to a floor entrance in Aja's chambers, as the trap door opened they over heard the guards outside the door, both maid and chauffeur scrambled around the room gathering all of the priestess' scrolls and stuffing them quickly into a large bag, Aja went to the table, opening a draw she pulled out a black leather bound book.

"Come we must go."

As she spoke, the door to the chamber flew open and two guards rushed in, Aja looked straight into their eyes and chanted throwing her hands in the air, both guards burst into flames, the priestess ushered her servants to open the trap door and they disappeared under ground.

The guards were screaming as the flames rose around them, they suddenly realised that the flames were not burning them at all, it was just an illusion. As the flames died down both guards flung the trap door open and pursued Aja. Numerous tunnels leading in different directions confused the guards as they did not know of their existence, they could faintly hear footsteps but were unsure of which tunnel to take, as they moved further down the east tunnel, they could hear something. There was something following them, they continued advancing and were now holding their weapons ready to strike if the situation required.

Each step they took, something moved too, they now walked back to back, prepared for an attack from any direction. A sinister growl coming from in front and behind them stopped them in their tracks. Without a second thought they both turned and fled towards the floor entrance in Aja's room. As they approached the trap door a loud roar ricocheted around the tunnel.

One of the guards managed to get into the room, he was just about to pull the other guard up from the tunnel, when with a swoop he was grabbed by the unknown creature and gone, a swift deathly cry surrounded the tunnel's walls. Aja looked back momentarily, laughing "I see they met my pets" she then ushered the maid and chauffeur to walk on, they were heading to the other side of the river where the carriage was waiting.

The guard quickly closed the door and lay on the floor catching his breath, still shaking with fright, as he moved his hand towards the lock, the trap door flung open throwing him across the room, springing out of the tunnel was the shedan, this grey, thick coated creature's fangs dripping with blood followed the motion of the guard. As he moved slowly the creature followed him in the same direction, gushing steam rose from its nostrils as the shedan snarled at the guard; he then realised that the creature could not see him but was attracted by sound.

The guard stood there with his heart in his mouth, his eyes searched rapidly around the chambers for something to defend himself with, his weapon had dropped when fleeing the tunnel, blood dripped from his cut brow and hit the chamber floor. He nervously looked down then straight up at the creature, the shedan pounced towards him, the guard manoeuvred as quickly as he could and flung himself towards the wall using his agility, he ran up the wall and swung himself onto the animal's back. With his bare hands he grabbed hold of its thick neck and punched his hand through the furry flesh.

The shedan roared in agony, tossing him violently around like he was a baby, the furniture smashed and splintered into pieces around the chamber. Blood poured from its neck, the guard had wounded the creature, in one swift movement the shedan gave out a ferocious roar and hurled the guard into the wall, smashing Aja's mirror.

Glass shattered everywhere, just as the creature was preparing for its final attack, the guard scrambled for a piece of the broken mirror and prepared to defend himself. At that moment the chamber's door swung open followed by firearms, blasting the shedan backwards, where it crumpled in a heap and took its last breath. The protectors swarmed into the room to aid the guard. He collapsed on the floor from exhaustion but was able to tell the protectors what had happened. Three of them jumped down into the dark tunnel; others stood waiting around the mouth of the hole while medics escorted the wounded guard out of the chamber.

Aja was safely in her carriage bound to Kianda, she set booby traps that exploded along the tunnel, leaving no way out other than through her room. As the bombs were detonated the ground shook, the tremor was felt around the palace quarters and within the city streets, the shriek of petrified baby sky lofful birds echoed in the skies as they flew in all directions in panic.

Over ground the warlord's sped towards the location of the bombs, as they checked the outer walls, they discovered the two dead handmaids along with the weapon, which was now identified as a Saggittan gun. The alarm was raised and the inner force field protecting the palace was programmed to its full potential, a message was sent to Lieutenant Sonkel on the finding of the weapon and dead maids. King Javari and the royal family along with servants were evacuated to a protective bunker within the palace. Warlords and protectors marched around checking possible threats to Nu Oarren, the north gate was now fully closed, no one could see in or out. A disabled device was found at the south gate, which distracted the guards from the direction Aja fled without detection. General Bakko and his guards found that it had been deactivated for a long time, one of the guards discovered a bag with robes and pieces of old decaying ban roots, Bakko realised this was where the Tau woman must have gained access, but that also meant that someone from the inside had let her in. Two protectors boarded their flyers and went through the damaged gate heading in different directions in the search of Aja. Officer Junn and the warlords were busy in the tetragon combat quarters; planning escape routes for the

King if an attack commenced. Underground some of the protectors found the remains of the unfortunate guard, they burnt it straight away to avoid contamination. Water could be heard above their heads which meant they were outside under the Ikediora river, with a growling roar the second shedan had found them but did not survive the skills of these soldiers.

Flying swiftly through the forest, the protectors soon picked up Aja's trail, the cloaked carriage manoeuvred in, under and around the roots of the great trees. One of the protectors signalled the other to split off. They both sailed past the invisible carriage, one protector dropped his hand to indicate their next move. A blue spray shot out from their weapons, the carriage began to solidify; the cloaking system started to deactivate, the carriage slowly became visible in the breaking dawn light and quickly descended onto the forest floor. Aja screamed with anger as the carriage suddenly came to a holt and both protectors walked over to the carriage, their weapons ready.

The chauffeur and maid threw their hands up in the air, signalling defeat. Aja was in a rage, she scouted for her weapon but could not see it, the captives were escorted out of the ship and stood there helpless. One of the protectors quickly covered them both with a field restraint to prevent her from doing anything

"we will have no more of your sorcery witch," Aja stared at the protector as he mocked her.

"You are our enemy priestess, you will die"

Both protectors walked around the felons. As they moved towards their captives a small craft came into view, it circled around the sky then shot off. They all looked up to the clouds to identify this unknown ship.

The protectors directed everyone to move under the shield of the trees, the craft flew back, but this time hovered lower to the ground near the carriage. The forest became silent, the protectors were armed and ready. The craft orbited the carriage then scanned it. Was this a new weapon device from the Nu Oarren army and the warlords? Suddenly four bright red lights shot out hitting the protectors, the maid and the chauffeur in their chests. Aja felt herself moving towards the craft, she turned to see the four bodies on the floor convulsing violently, wrapped in a red beaming blanket of net. Her body pivoted from vertical to horizontal by the invisible force pulling her towards the craft, she was drawn into the back of the craft along with her scrolls and books, the door closed, and the ship sped off at an alarming speed into the morning skies.

--- CHAPTER 16 ---

THE SPY

The suns began to rise as Murrock docked near the hut, she had fallen asleep, it was the sweetest sleep she had had for a long time, Nyper was snuggled in the bag still fast asleep. The warrior unwrapped the bag of ban roots and entered the room, Gogo was sitting around the table, she whispered

"they still sleep, come."

They both walked into the old woman's quarters. Gogo laughed as she walked around Murrock

"Oh you do look a sight" even the warrior chuckled too.

"Let me see" Murrock opened the bag revealing Nyper.

"Oh, she is beautiful"

Gogo lifted her out of the bag and placed her in a little bed she had prepared. Gogo gave a chuckling smile at Murrock's attempt to swaddle the child.

"You did this?" gesturing towards the torn robe, the warrior grunted to regain her dignity.

"Now this, this is good my warrior. I see that you will make a fine mother," Gogo smiled and chuckled again. Murrock grunted a second time but with a slight smile.

"Do not wonder warrior I know many things, one thing I know for sure; you must wash with haste" Gogo fanned her nose and ushered Murrock to her room

"we will talk later, rest Murrock."

The embarrassed warrior ambled towards her sleeping quarters. The old woman looked down at Nyper and stroked her head

"your mother was beautiful, just like you my little one. You will do great things and your new mother Murrock shall shelter you from any harm."

Gogo recalled Lani-ma spending time with her before she left for Bernal, she also remembered both Lani-ma and Murrock in combat training when they were youngsters. Gogo smiled from her heart and began to sing an ancient lullaby as she steadily rocked the cradle. The old woman knew many things but could not reveal them until it was time. As the child slept, Gogo rummaged around looking for a certain scroll, she pulled things out from one place and pushed scrolls into another place, all the animals in the hut scurried out of her way. Gogo muttered as she searched high and low,

"Ahh" Gogo found what she was looking for

"I would never have found you."

The old woman stopped for a second and looked up; something was moving at light speed across the distant skies, murmuring again she sat down gazing at the scroll.

"Tomorrow" Gogo said quietly as her fingers moved back to rock the cradle.

***

By now more surveillance teams of protectors had reached the forest and found their comrades, they were able to disarm the net and release their men, the chauffeur and the maid were shackled and taken into a ship bound for the dark chambers. Hundreds of warlords marched around the grounds of the palace in search of anything suspicious; King Javari was safely hidden along with Queen Adama and other family members. No one slept much that ashshun and now that dawn was upon them, they sat heavy in debate.

"And you feel Javari, this is all the work of one-person Priestess Aja?" Sonkel paced around the room perplexed by what was being divulged in the quarters.

"My blood runs with a bitter taste, to know Aja is to blame, she puts everyone at risk especially our Empress, but why would she do this?"

The King sat beside Adama gently holding her hand.

"Nothing shall come of this; the prophecy shall live." Sonkel

turned around quickly

"pray cousin what! What is this of the prophecy?"

The King sighed,

"Not now Sonkel,"

"Javari how can you speak such a thing? You still believe in this nonsense, you are a wise King my cousin but to rely on this to save your kingdom and the planet is ludicrous, we must war, our fathers died in battle to protect our kingdom over this stupid prophecy!"

Tension flooded into the room, Sonkel threw his hands up in despair, his father Rufus had not returned with King Agu and was declared dead, Sonkel was enraged, he threw himself into a chair banging his hands on the table. Javari stood up with his father's memory blazing through his body and stared into Sonkel's eyes, bellowing and nostrils flaring

"I am the King! And I say the prophecy, shall be fulfilled!"

The room fell deathly quiet, everyone stared at Javari whose eyes were still fixed firmly on his cousin, Sonkel shamefully bowed his head quietly apologising to him, then spoke amongst his brothers Junn and Bakko, Javari gradually calmed down enough to join in and continue with the discussion of preparing for an attack.

They quickly began to execute ideas of battle tactics and plans to deploy the army. Swearing an allegiance to revenge all those who dared attack the Solomon family, the cousins soon forgot the previous temperament in the room. Javari stood and invited Queen Adama to walk with him. He questioned her more about her prediction and whether he could truly keep his faith in this legend. A hopeful tone slipped from her mouth

"My son, fear not we must be strong for her, we must continue to believe, it is essential. I was born to hold the leckon bracelet until this crucial moment, reasons are not all clear, but we must be faithful, the sisters knew why they did what they did."

The King nodded giving a semi cheerful smile. Just then the warlords entered the protected zone to inform the King that the guardians are at the sacred mount and awaited him. Javari gave a signal then left the room followed by Foruth and Dacken, Sonkel and Bakko trailed behind him bound for the west gate to the sacred mount's cave.

--- CHAPTER 17 ---

REUNION

Although Aja was freed from the captivity of the protectors her fate was now in the hands of these unknown rebels. The craft had docked into the belly of a larger ship, she sensed it had landed due to the sudden jerking motion then stillness to a rocking sensation. The soldiers transported her from the craft into an elevator, then freed her from the restraints and left her standing with her bags and books. The door opened, prompting her to move forward, the door closed leaving the priestess standing in what seemed to be a battle room. Large maps spanned the walls, unknown devices were spread across a huge metal table, bulky glass windows surrounded half of the room, Aja could see the sea front of the Umi ocean she knew these waters well from her training, the ship was heading east to the city of Kargel.

From the corner of her eye she noticed a man propped on a chair; one leg up and one on the floor, dressed in combat green armour, his face was covered with a metal mask. Cautiously he approached Aja then circled around her a few times. The priestess followed the man with her eyes, slowly putting her books in her bag, she was preparing to fight if she had to and was waiting for his next move. As Aja inspected his attire, she saw the imperial markings on his uniform of Kargel, was this Commander Grave? He was close enough for her to grab to read him or even cast an illusion, but she hesitated as she was unsure what weapons he may be hiding. The man then stood beside her and whispered into her ear

"What do you know of the prophecy?" The concealed voice echoed behind the mask. Aja side-eyed the man, mystified to know the identity of the stranger, his voice was not familiar, nor his scent.

"I speak of nothing, who are you?"

The priestess was riddled with anger; her heart was racing but she kept her focus on staying in control and continued talking with confidence.

"I", the man gave out a humiliating chuckle and continued pacing around Aja.

This intimidation annoyed the priestess, it angered her because she did not know what to expect from this man.

"You have great strength I see; this is good we can work with this."

The priestess glared at the offensive man, was this all an elaborate test by the guardians? As the figure moved closer to her once more, he paused for a moment, the crashing sound of the sea hitting the hull of the ship and the clanging of the engines overpowered the silence for a moment. Aja kept still, unsure of his next move, step by step he moved closer to her then said

"I" he paused again, Aja's heart was thumping in her chest, who was this man? And what did he want from her?

"I'm..." He paused once more.

Aja could not control her temper and bare another word from his lips, she was now fuming she screamed out

"who are you?"

The man stepped back gazing into her eyes and said,

"I am, I am your Husband"

"Duke?"

Aja's mouth uttered his name, but it was a reaction not a response. The man took his time to unmask himself, revealing his face, it was Duke; badly disfigured on the left side of his handsome face from the torturing ordeal of the dark chambers but still recognisable, now cut short long gone was his mane of silky blonde hair, Aja's eyes widened but did not blink, her jaw dropped in disbelief and her head started spinning, she gripped her chest as it tightened from losing her breath she collapsed in a heap to the floor. Scrambling to her aid he knelt beside her, slowly raising her head up after she hit it on the floor, he lifted her into his arms while she came around from fainting. As her eyes slowly met his, they were emotionless; something was now missing from the imperial officer, he seemed soulless. The quietness soon became drowned out by a hysterical scream.

The priestess now in shock started trembling, tears flooded down her cheeks, nervous sweat appeared on Duke's brow as he waited for her to say something. He repeated her name, a distorted voice echoed in her head, she could not believe that her husband was before her, holding her, speaking to her after almost two and half lucas, he was not dead. He spoke again but calmed his approach

"it's me Aja, it's me" still peering into his eyes she took a deep breath then struck him firmly across his face,

"you left me for dead!"

Aja's blood was boiling, she was right to doubt the guards and Javari, she knew they were lying, she just knew, and her hunch was right; her husband lived. Aja's head hung down, in a faint voice gripped by sorrow she turned to Duke

"how could you have done this to me? Our... our son," her eyes glowed white as she held onto Duke, she then saw imprints of the past in a flash of what really happened that ashshun and all that the imperial officer was involved with, as her sighting ventured deeper. He quickly pulled her hands away from him

"stop. You will only hurt yourself."

The priestess edged away from him and got to her feet leaving Duke still kneeling.

"Why did you do this? We could have left Nu Oarren together, why didn't you come for me? I thought you were dead,"

Aja briskly moved towards the ship's window, staring out to the sea, she shouted out

"for power? For power over Tau? For control?"

Duke quickly got to his feet but remained at a snail's pace approaching his wife, he hesitated when she looked back and made sure not to stand too close to her.

"Forgive me, this was the only way, it has taken over two lucas to be ready," he pleaded

"you have no idea of what you put me through, do you?" Aja spat back.

He took two more steps closer

"I had to endure seeing them every yante! Salivating in their joy, while I suffered in silence and kept to my duties! I was your wife! You left us and you are telling me this was a plan? Did you plan for our child!"

Duke remained silent but moved even closer to her,

"our son, where were you for me Duke?"

The priestess stormed across the room to sit on the chair and tried to make sense of everything.

"Aja, Aja, I had no choice, this was the only way I could revenge our honour" he stumbled.

"Honour, honour Duke? Stop this, stop this I cannot take any more of your..."

"Aja, I have something for you."

Reluctantly Aja turned to face Duke, to see what he had for her. Slowly standing and steadying her balance; she was still dizzy from the shock and buried pain stirring in her soul.

"Wasn't it you that always said they were not strong enough to govern Kemi?" He asked,

"but you completely missed the point Duke, I was still content, I understood my duties and place!"

"Aja, I wasn't! Didn't you see that Aja? You didn't see me; didn't you sight me?" Duke beat upon his chest in rage

"I did this for us!" Quickly turning on her heels she was now face to face

"Please don't try and turn this around, this battle you cannot win, you destroyed everything, do you know who I have become through this?"

Grabbing hold of his lapels, the priestess pulled Duke wanting to throw him to the ground, he gently held her arms moving them slowly down.

"Can you forgive me? I saved you from their clutches" he pleaded again "but this was all because of you!"

The priestess held her head once again, she felt faint

"let me rest somewhere, I need to lay down, I need a moment"

"I will get Cruel to take you to your quarters, but first" Duke turned back gesturing someone to come forward.

A pale sinister looking woman with bright purple hair tied in two large plaits entered the room, holding on to the hand of a striking child, the woman was dressed in a green leather body suit with thigh high combat boots. The young boy stood dressed in a miniature version of the officer's combat clothing. Aja turned to see the child and was distracted for a moment by the piercing stare coming from this strange woman. Her heart began to race as the boy stepped towards her, step by step he moved closer, her eyes glanced from the boy to the woman who was now turning to walk away. He reached out and gently held her shaking hand. Duke walked closer towards Aja and stood behind her saying quietly,

"this is Kabbastian, our new son."

As the woman closed the door smirking

"Duke maybe it wasn't good idea" He raised his eyebrows in possible agreement, but it was too late.

The priestess stood in bewilderment; her forehead wrinkled with astonishment from what Duke had said.

"Our son, Kabbastian?" Aja turned her face staring deep into the imperial officer's eyes

"how can this be?" clenching her jaws she gnashed her teeth, fury rushed through her body, her heart was thumping.

"Our... our child is dead!" screamed the priestess.

Aja angrily flung her hand away toppling the boy to the ground and staggered across the room embracing the window for balance.

"Get me out of here! Get me out of here!" she demanded.

"Wait Aja, please my love" Aja looked back towards Duke, love, she had not heard those words said to her for so long

"Your timing is pathetic! even that leather wrapped walking boot knew you were wrong! How could you possibly believe I would embrace this?"

her finger pointed to the child who was now getting to his little feet, the Officer was speechless again he assumed it would have gone differently and had forgotten how emotional his wife could be, but this was an exceptional circumstance which he had failed to plan for wisely. He had to turn things around for Aja was the next key to finding the scrolls.

"I, I am sorry Aja, I am so sorry, can you ever forgive me? I knew of your pain, word was sent to me, Aja wait, listen. I don't know how you feel, you are right, your loss our loss was great, I am incapable of changing what has happened I take the blame, this is our chance to change our life course, to start again, stay with me as we crush and destroy Nu Oarren. The prophecy shall not live in their hands, we will conquer this planet, Javari is weak we can take the throne, he still lied to you and Subira they didn't include you with the truth when all you did was give them truth!"

"You know"

Aja quietly answered him, both Duke and the child stood waiting for her response,

"are you mad Duke? If it wasn't for my rank and order, you would have never been an officer, did you marry me for a greater position? Did you? Did you Duke? Did you?" Aja screamed at her husband, the unfearful child eagerly watched them both full of intrigue and excitement at their displays.

The priestess became stone cold with rage her eyes poured tears of anger and sadness, rubbing her brow she cupped her face with her hands to try and ease the pain. Her thoughts leapt back in time remembering the yante the news of her husband's death was announced, how she became ill and then sent to Camu hills for healing and finally tragically losing her first born, then spending one and a half lucas in mourning and alone.

Her tears fell slowly and travelled around the circles on her cheeks. The priestess, although a royal pure seer, was poisoned from the depths of her soul after her double loss. This chain of events compelled her to defy her high priestess order by unlocking the forbidden scrolls and learning of their immense powers she had manipulated a priest who helped her to learn as much as she could before returning to Nu Oarren. Aja could not bear the thought of raising a child to replace her own, but she now had her Duke back. Her mind franticly raced around seeing flashes of images of the last two yantes, the sighting, the guardians, her husband. Gradually her angry thoughts subsided her purpose had changed, she was out of her depth, but the priestess took back control of her emotions. Acknowledging that she could still turn things around for the betterment of herself she numbed her heart, wiped the last tears that fell and stared out to the seas. Aja stood still only moving her hand towards the window to steady her balance, not a sound came from her not a word she just stood there for what seemed like many, many hibbs. Duke dared not interrupt her silent cries, a slow-moving Kabbastian headed over towards Aja, carefully reaching out to her hand while looking at her face, he waited for her to box it away again, but this time she held onto it.

The priestess still stood silent, Duke took his time to join them near the window, he stood at the opposite side of her and held her other hand, he too waited for her to throw his hand away, but she squeezed it more tightly. The Imperial Officer her husband Duke was alive, Aja turned and looked down at Kabbastian, then turned to look at Duke. Both Duke and Kabbastian glanced at each other, the child was about to speak but Duke quickly shook his head urging him to keep quiet. This moment was so surreal, she now had a new family, at last it seemed that some of her sightings were unfolding, it was now slowly making sense and fate had brought about this union. Nu Oarren, Javari, Subira and the prophecy would fall and fall into her hands. A tiny smile seeped from the corner of her mouth, her mind settled within itself, the joy of revenge blossomed in her heart, this time she was not alone, she couldn't have planned it better if she had tried, this time she could be on the right side to complete the prophecy and keep the power, it was so much more than revenge it was floorless.

--- CHAPTER 18 ---

THE PLOT

At the west gate cave of the palace, in the sacred mount, the guardians stood alone with the King. They spoke and warned him of many plots against his throne and kingdom. The West gate was the last place Javari saw his father, he and his uncle disappeared at the battle of Aluke, never to be seen again, it was rumoured they died, but had never been confirmed, until Queen Adama revealed what she had witnessed. The guardians revealed to Javari that Aja had used her ordained powers to manipulate the King in his sleep. Her powers gave her authority over water and inanimate objects, by using her mirror she was able to connect with his subconscious mind and spirit; drawing information from him so she could formulate her vengeful plan.

This all made sense to the King, many ashshuns he had felt himself disturbed and remembered having vivid dreams of dimensions and hearing a familiar voice, he had thought it was all part of the prophecy or a terrible nightmare. The guardians gave Javari a vessel containing sands from Aluke and was told what to do with it and when. The guardians were unable to see all that was to unfold, but they saw the final battle and where it would take place.

The King was also given instructions to leave Nu Oarren a camala before the birth of his child and unite with his wife. Waiting in the doorway of the mount stood Javari's two cousins, they were questioning the whereabouts of the Empress.

"She is safe" Javari returned from the mount and answered them

"I must return to the quarters and speak with Adama alone."

His cousins bowed and parted from the King. As they walked away, Sonkel turned back to watch the King leave; worrying for his cousin. Although Javari was surrounded by his warriors, he felt alone as they marched down the corridors, he felt more concern for his wife and child's life. As far as the citizens and servants of Nu Oarren knew, Empress Subira was still within the palace walls and safe. The King had to keep up appearances to avoid any double agents discovering his wife's true whereabouts.

***

Everyone was awake in the hut as the bright sunrays descending from the heavens broke the morning mist, Gogo and her servants prepared the table for the morning feasts. Subira undoing her long black locks and shaking them free was now feeling more comfortable and rested after hearing the news that her husband was fine. As she sat at the table and reached for a piece of fruit, she felt something touch her feet, she peeped under the table to see what it was. There, playing with a protector's helmet was Nyper. As Subira spoke softly to the creature, Murrock walked into the room and saw the Empress reaching for Nyper.

"Your Highness, please no!!"

The warrior ran over to save Subira from the antics of Nyper but tumbled to the ground tripping over pots and pans the child had left on the floor, before she could get there Nyper scrambled up the Empress' leg and sat on her lap,

Murrock covered her face, fearing that Nyper would unleash another deadly present.

"Isn't this creature beautiful, I think it's a female" Subira stroked Nyper's head and the child snuggled close to her stomach. Gogo peered at them both

"She knows you carry a child."

"How, how can this be?"

"My Empress the Tau can sense many things; can't you tell how she cuddles close to your belly." Subira smiled embracing the creature

"what is her name?" Murrock paused, reluctantly answering Subira

"hmm Nyper, my Empress."

"Nyper, you are stunning," the child smiled, peeked over at Murrock and stuck her tongue out teasing her then gave the Empress a cheeky grin. The warrior rolled her eyes and got to her feet grunting. Gogo strolled over to the Empress holding a vessel containing a special juice.

"Empress you must drink this, it will be good for you and your child."

Murrock advanced to take the drink, the old woman stared at her signalling that it was safe. As Subira drank the liquid Nyper sat up begging for some. The Empress gave the child the last sip, the old woman was about to stop her then halted briefly watching the child's reaction, she held the cup taking every last drop. Gogo toddled off towards the kitchen muttering. The Empress' and Nyper's eyes closed and they sat still for a moment. Cautiously the protectors and Murrock watched until their eyes opened.

"This is good, I feel so lovely and peaceful and warm inside, is there anymore?" Subira stood up holding Nyper in her arms, the faint voice of Gogo came from the kitchen

"no, no my Empress."

Walking through the doors of the hut Subira was greeted by the sun's rays and sweet scents dancing in the air of Nu Jahri. As she stood at the balcony, the protectors marched out beside her, she turned to both sides signalling to them to give her some space. Gazing out to the ulowpillors their calls seemed different; each creature swam not away but towards her. Nyper looked out from her snuggled position as the creatures began to croon an alluring heavenly sound, which echoed around the sea and huts. The protectors, handmaids and Murrock hurried out to see this amazing sight, the natives of Nu Jahri all stopped their daily activities as they heard this enchanting sound. Standing in wondrous silence they witnessed something miraculous before their eyes.

The glistening scales of the creatures shivered and rattled but it was so mystifying it made the waters vibrate. Gogo looked out of the kitchen window as she groomed the thick brown fur of one of her animals, she smiled knowing that the prophecy was materialising. Murrock ran into the kitchen alerting Gogo of the unexplained event that she was witnessing.

"Gogo what is this?" asked the uncertain warrior.

"Murrock"

Gogo continued brushing her pet and collecting its fur in a wooden bowl, the animal peered from the side of its eyes and growled at Murrock for disturbing its grooming.

"The Empress carries peace over many provinces and galaxies, this child you must train and prepare for battle, what you see is the beginning of a new world, the outcome I do not know, but the birth is true and loss will be great."

Murrock gazed at the old woman as her answer was a little thick and she would have preferred a simpler reply.

"You Murrock will unlearn, now leave my warrior, so I can prepare." Murrock bowed and left, even more puzzled than she was before speaking to Gogo.

As Murrock appeared on the balcony Subira held onto Murrock's arm and placed her hand over her round stomach.

"The child is kicking, feel."

The warrior reluctantly allowed the Empress to guide her hand over her stomach. Murrock's eyes opened in astonishment as the baby kicked twice, she looked at Subira gleaming with delight. Murrock said in a firm voice

"strong" and Subira chuckled with joy.

The ulowpillors now gracefully swam around the waters close to the hut, the shimmering had stopped but the submerged crooning continued for many hibbs. The Empress cuddled Nyper who had now fallen asleep in her arms, as Subira walked back into the hut a protector was summoned again to contact the King.

"Take this to Gogo, she will tell you where to go."

The protector was handed the Empress' brooch, embedded in its centre was a green emerald similar to her husband's bead that hung from his beard. The protector headed to the kitchen then left shortly after to the messenger shrine to contact the King once more. The shrine walls were covered with orgonite, this healing stone blocked any interception of corrupt energies from Islands near Nu Jahri. Although the closest islands were almost seventeen hibbs away they had to ensure security with their communication.

--- CHAPTER 19 ---

KARGEL

Saggitta and the Volker trackers teamed up to spy on and collect information about the plots of Commander Grave and his clan. They were now the main suspect for the raid on the weaponry room. The trackers had now reached the outskirts of the metal city of Kargel where they believe information could be gained about the current plans of Commander Grave. This settlement was overflowing with monstrous skyscrapers and thick foliage that coiled around the huge monuments of their leader like frozen creatures. The most notorious criminals, the wildest of wild families' and petty thieves inhabited this unorthodox domain. They traded metal and any other material that could be used for construction of buildings, ships or even weaponry.

This city is in its infancy stage and was built over ten lucas. It is said that Commander Grave had visited the planet Kemi and traded a large sum of money for the land of Kargel with the villagers. He, along with his female accomplice and wife lady Cruel began to construct the monstrous mechanical metropolis that now stood. He came with great wealth but from where? No-one really knew of his origin but knew of his wrath as he afflicted it upon anyone who defied him or his wife.

The Commander's rein gradually spread through Kemi like a dreadful virus; claiming land by payment or by force from weaker tribes that could not defend themselves against his iron grip; targeting lands that contained metals. This increased authority was becoming a planetary threat and soon enemies joined forces to prevent the invasion of this wicked man. People living within the walls of Kargel soon became jealous of this stranger's power, fractions broke away creating subdivisions: there was never honour amongst thieves. It wasn't too long until the underworld robbers began to bargain amongst themselves; trading secrets of the city to the highest bidder.

The Saggitta and Volker soldiers obtained some attack plans from Kargel, they were leaked to the island of Kianda then sold on to the trading village of Bernal. Trackers from the Saggitta clan overheard an argument in the tavern where two petty thieves were bickering about who they should sell the information to: Etha, Mataina or somewhere further away or just keep them for their own use. A brawl broke out as the two drunken soldiers fought one another over the attention of a Gep woman, one of the trackers took this opportunity to snatch the blueprints; whilst pretending to stop the fight. He passed them quickly to a Volker tracker, who cleverly stole their uniforms, they made a swift exit and headed towards Kargel.

The blueprints displayed rough drafts of the development of new technology, next to the signature of Commander Grave, some territories were circled; indicating attack plans. Stuck to three of the corners of one blueprint were fragments taken from old scrolls relating to the prophecy. The men looked over the plans and found two possible entrance and exit routes then prepared to enter the City.

Dressed in Kargel uniforms they followed the path towards the murky underground drainage system. This path led them close to the main weaponry building, three other warriors; two from Volker and one more from Saggitta had rendezvoused as planned and lay waiting at the entrance for the two men's return.

The thick salty moisture in the air of Kargel affected the body of the Saggitta tracker, not used to this climate it made his sweat have a faint colouring of pale blue. Walking further into the building, they both could see defects from their own tribes, but it was obvious they had been there for a long time, with their out of shape bodies and overgrown hair, they seemed more like prisoner's.

They blended in with the other workers, they moved in and out of the building following other men lifting cargo.

"You two!" a guard beckoned them over to a holding bay,

"and you and you." The four men walked towards him,

"Go down to the sub room, it requires more men, quickly now!"

The two warriors followed the other two men to a lift, they were in luck. Soon they would see for themselves what machinery lay in the belly of Kargel and hopefully would find evidence connecting Grave to the robbery and think of a way to sabotage the plans should they be true and protect their tribes.

--- CHAPTER 20 ---

THE KING

Meanwhile back at the palace, King Javari completed the communication with the protector, he refastened the bead back to his beard. The bead was placed into a holding channel which connected to a solar device, it in turn sent out light images that could be audible and visible in small bursts. Once the protector placed the Empress' brooch into a socket within one of the stones it gave out a pulse that alerted the King by his bead. The bead changed colour which drew the attention of the King and signalled him to return to the sacred mount, to access the messenger receiver.

Javari informed the protector of the previous hibb's events and the King was given positive news on the Empress' state and pregnancy. After this communication Javari went to share with the Queen Mother the news of her daughter. Adama was delighted to hear her daughter was safe and further changes had begun.

Javari requested that Adama should be taken to her daughter despite the royal protocol of separation of mother and daughter during the second trimester. The guards, warlords and protectors filled the palace grounds as no further devices or threats were detected, which gave a clear and safe signal to move the Queen quickly.

The protector was asked to inform the Empress that her mother would be joining her. King Javari requested the presence of his three cousins Sonkel, Junn and Bakko.

"You are to accompany the Queen to Nu Jahari as royal ambassadors, please keep my family safe"

" No Javari!, I will stay with you, the others can go, Aja still lurks and no one can be trusted, this is my duty to you my King" Sonkel stated.

"Sonkel, I agree, please stay." Bakko nodded

"Junn and I will go, we will guard them with our lives, fear not Javari we will protect our bloodline and kin."

Javari summoned Foruth placed a small vile in his hand, Foruth nodded, turned and left.

Holding onto each other; gripping their forearms, like when they were children. The cousins all spoke the words together

"to the bond of Solomon."

Javari ordered any of the Royal family left within the palace were to be taken to safe locations across Kemi, he also requested that the noblemen should post and imprint of the Empress with him, as he walked through the palace grounds he knew he could not leave Nu Oarren until the last yante, the final camala before his child's birth. Queen Adama, her guards and handmaidens along with Bakko and Junn now dressed in Nu Jahri robes, assembled at the docking gates awaiting departure.

--- CHAPTER 21 ---

AJA AND CRUEL

The ashshun had fallen on the path of Aja's destination after two yantes, they had now reached Kargel. The ship docked into a large metal mouth carved in the image of its ruler, as it entered the watery chambers the mouth closed behind them. The surroundings were polluted by the smell of thick oil and the clanging of tools, patter of slave's feet and workers busy repairing the ships poisoned the air. The fleet was quite small and dotted sporadically along the middle of the vessel. Aja with her husband and Kabbastian were escorted into a lift, she gazed around this monumental metal shell.

Lady Cruel followed behind, carrying a case containing more blueprints. They arrived at sector three, the doors opened revealing Commander Grave along with two foot soldiers and Coalbolt the head of the assassin clan. Commander Grave's bold blue piercing eyes connected to the priestess' green eyes. he had a pale but lightly tanned complexion, standing tall in a green uniform. A distinctive cap rested upon his thick black hair and covering his shoulders was a piped valve armour construction that emitted tiny bubbling sounds. Aja broke her gaze while he took off the contraption, removing his gloves while strolling up to his wife; embracing her in a passionate kiss, her eyes peered back at Aja as she walked off with Kabbastian leaving the case on a table. The priestess' eyes wandered around looking at his guards sweating profusely, she nudged her husband gesturing towards the men,

"he has arthritis" Duke pointed to his left shoulder,

"he makes his close men wear armour too, so he does not feel embarrassed"

"Can't they turn the heat a dial down? They look feverish" it was the first time for a long time that both Duke and Aja really giggled, her smile slowly faded as Grave approached her, carefully watched by Duke, opening his arms he greeted her with a short embrace.

"Welcome to Kargel Priestess, our home is your home." He guided them to sit amongst his footmen and Coalbolt.

"We have infiltrators within these walls, it impresses me to know they have the guts to try and defy me." Grave laughed as he opened the case; revealing plans of another attack.

"We know of the forbidden scrolls, they are kept in Camu, do you know of their chambers?" Aja was shocked by his direct questioning, peering at her husband she slowly nodded,

"I know of many chambers and scrolls, what is it you desire Commander?"

The priestess was well aware of Grave's request but by her true nature she mocked his superiority. The Commander stared hard into Aja's eyes

"we know of the defence of the hill but my sources inform me that in four camalas it can be penetrated" he gazed at her almost waiting for a lie to seep out of her mouth, Aja paused and gave a long drawn out answer.

"Yes... this is true," she could feel the anticipation of everyone and thought cunningly on her reply.

"I can guide the attack if you grant me this opportunity of revenge Commander!"

Grave laughed even louder and stood up slamming his hands on the table.

"I like you!! Your wife, she reminds me of Cruel," his chuckle bounced around the metal walls, tossing his hands in the air he spun around like a lunatic. Aja noticed a tattoo at the nape of his neck and wanted to ask him what it meant as abrupt as he questioned her.

"This is our time, we take, we break, we conquer! Bring food, we must eat! Then high priestess we will talk of this prophecy"

Grave was very aware that his artillery could not attack as planned, until he had in his possession, the wisdom of the priestess. She knew of the whereabouts of some or all of the Autom scrolls and they would give him the immense power he so desired, not only over Kemi but other planets too. The timing had to be perfect for him to win; patience and planning were essential. Slaves scurried into the room carrying trays of food and bottles of wine, Aja looked at the food in disgust, she had lived a privileged life in Nu Oarren and would never eat such peasant foods, but hunger outweighed her rejection of this meagre display. Grave grabbed hold of a jelly substance gobbling it up quickly, wiping his mouth with the back of his hand. His handsome face seemed ugly as his table manners unimpressed the priestess.

***

The two trackers had managed to penetrate sector five by volunteering to move cargo to the upper deck of this mechanical layer. As they walked along the quarters, imprints were taken and fed back to the alliance. From one of the rooms they could hear painful screams of people, they looked into this room as the door was ajar and saw a group of Tau women chained together and were being prodded with a light stick by a sinister looking woman. They continued moving the heavy cargo on floating plates into the lifts to move to a higher sector. Suddenly the door swung open and Lady Cruel stepped out, looked left and right down the hallway, she was about to return into the room, but noticed something glowing on the floor, quickly bending down she cautiously touched the patch and brought it up to her nose. A screech escaped her lips and caused two guards to rush out the room to see what had happened. A button was pressed and in a tali, the floor was soon full of guards who were given commands from Cruel, they raced in different directions towards the lifts. Cruel sent a signal from her belt device which alerted Commander Grave. With a smug smile he bit his lip

"We must leave Duke, it seems their luck of stealing from me has run out, they were not so careful after all, come."

They both stood leaving Aja sitting amongst the blueprints and Coalbolt, she took her time to gaze over the plans and took everything in whilst keeping an eye on the others in the room.

Luck had struck, the two warriors entered a room stumbling upon more evidence of the Commander's scheme, plots were outlined on smaller plans, the weaponry from the Saggitta tribe and their battling gear were now adapted and would be used to plot an invasion over territory lines. They read of a scheme that was to frame the Saggitta and the Volker kin and leave them at the heart of the conspiracy. This plot would forge a war against each tribe; creating a divide and breaking the stronghold that both kinsmen had throughout Kemi and Nu Oarren. The Saggittan tracker noticed a screen where areas of the Volker land were circled indicating the possible locations of the scrolls.

As they continued scanning the plans, they both stopped in shock, there lay a treaty between the Saggitta King Skylan and Grave

"do you know what this means?"

"Yes, your people are the traitors"

"No this cannot be true, King Skylan would never do this to us, this must be a forgery"

"forged!! My King was right all along, it was your kin greedy for power, what makes you think this is not true? Skylan has sold us out, I see it in your eyes, the doubt you have for your own King."

A heaviness overcame his body as he looked down at the treaty, immobilized for a second as the Volker tracker stood fuming with the thought of betrayal. Raging forward he grabbed the Saggittan tracker when the door to sector six swung open revealing a swarm of guards followed closely by Lady Cruel. Realising they had been discovered both men quickly looked around for an escape route, ahead of them was a tight stairwell which seemed to be their only option. Grabbing as much as they could from the table they hurried to get out. Dodging blasts from the weapons of the guards, they darted up the stairs unsure of where it would lead them. Around and around the stairs spiralled, they could hear the guards on their heels, the stairs went around until they reached a metal door, it was fastened tight, but both pulled frantically at the rusty handle until it gave way; opening into the upper deck. They fought through the whistling sea breeze, searching for the safest escape route. They were just about to jump from the deck when a blast came out of nowhere, hitting the Saggittan tracker square in the chest, launching him across the floor. Using his solar surge, the Volker tracker blasted as many guards out of their path as he could, running back for the Saggittan tracker he grabbed his bag with the plans and dragged him to his feet. They scurried between empty cargo containers; avoiding the blasts from the guards. The Volker tracker saw an opening at the edge of the ship, he fastened the bag to his back and was about to jump holding his comrade. When suddenly he felt a thousand kicks, this broke his grip on the Saggittan man; hurtling him to the floor. Without hesitation he dived overboard, disappearing into the mist of the sea front; taking the plans with him.

A disappointed squeal came from the mist, Lady Cruel stretched her neck over the ship trying to see if she could see where the intruder had landed but there was no sign. Turning back, she watched the Saggittan man trying to get to his feet, she flipped her body into the air springing on him and pinning him down. Her hands signalled the guards to find the other infiltrator, in that tali the Saggittan man spun her from on top of him launching her over his head into a container. Holding his chest in pain, he tried desperately to release his energy wings, but the salty air did not make it easy. The light began to glow a little stronger when Cruel flew through the air, toppling him to the floor. One of the guards was about to blast him

"Noooo, let me play, oh let me play, move back!" Cruel mused.

Wiping away a little blood from her lips, she shook with excitement to battle this warrior. Dancing around smiling, Cruel watched as he staggered to his feet, with two flips and twists spinning into the air she fly kicked the warrior into the cargo, he blasted her with his light force, which was getting stronger, but she spun out of its way. The guards circled around them pointing their weapons towards him. He got to his feet preparing to fight for his life, Cruel shrugged her shoulders and faced the tracker ready to fight.

The two opponents fought hand-to-hand combat; kick after kick, punch after punch. Cruel laughed as she battled with him. The tracker pulled his hands together and pushed an air ball of light, hurling it towards Cruel. Her speed wasn't enough and was shocked by the light, crippling her to the floor. Fighting off the light she pressed her wristband which contained a weapon that disabled the light instantly. As she started to run towards him, he released another blast skidding her across the wet deck floor, she quickly got up, wiping herself down, indicating his attack was poor. More soldiers came running into position to attack and capture the warrior.

Cruel screamed out "wait"

as the tracker was about to fire off another blast, spinning around she created a shock wave from her device, that blasted him almost unconscious. The guards quickly covered their ears to try and block the pain from the noise. Cruel quickly released a red net caging device, covering the tracker.

Struggling to regain his balance through the net, she gloated over him; dusting off her leather boots and with one strong swift side kick she knocked him out cold. Commander Grave and Duke arrived at the upper deck to see Cruel standing over the body of the perpetrator.

"Bring the body, take him to the cells" the Commander strolled up to his wife with pride, kissing her on her forehead and wiping her mouth

"how did you know my love?"

"I sensed someone at my door and noticed a blot of blue water on the clear floor, I've seen this before when the first defectors from the Saggitta came to Kargel, I followed my intuition"

Grave snickered "your intuition served you well."

Duke helped the guards carry off the tracker.

"One got away with our blueprints Grave" informed Cruel

"sound the alarm and release the sky troops, he cannot have gone far, get Coalbolt's assassins on the ground and find out what is missing." Grave ordered

"I sent some guards ahead" Cruel responded

"good, we will soon have him."

Fortune was on the side of the Volker tracker, he was able to move unseen back to the underground drainage, meeting the other trackers at the entrance. He was badly wounded from escaping, grabbing the bag off his back, they carried him off; disappearing into the misty morning.

--- CHAPTER 22 ---

TRADITIONS

Subira could not sleep that ashshun as she knew her mother had been given permission to come to Nu Jahri, she sat in a tall bamboo chair on the balcony waiting for her mother's arrival. Joined by the protectors and little Nyper she held onto the thick rope bridge looking out to the sea, Nyper mimicked the crooning of the ulowpillors, whose calls were now faint. Murrock and the other warriors were seated around the table playing the ancient game of Meji. This five-level game was commonly played for training intuition. It consisted of small panels that moved around and changed their places, each player must return their ball back to the last level, whilst detecting their opponents ball hidden behind the panels and destroy it.
Gogo toddled up to the Empress

"You must be pleased that your mother is coming."

"Why yes it gives me great pleasure to know I will have her here with me, not that I don't feel comfortable with you Gogo."

"My child have no fear, you must understand that this is breaking custom, to be separated from your mother in this time allows you to bond."

"Why should a King not be able to change protocol?"

Gogo giggled through a nod "indeed Empress in-deed."

"My child has been kicking more often since I drank your juice, pray, tell me what did it contain?"

Gogo stared at the ground for a moment, thinking

"It is to bring harmony to your wellbeing Empress, let us walk."

Two protectors followed the party along the bridge, Murrock peered over as they wandered along but did not follow the party, behind them Nyper strutted along imitating the protectors, sniggering with herself.

"What do you know of the prophecy Gogo, very little was explained to mean until now."

"Hmmm, it will change many things within and out" the Empress looked puzzled with her answer.

"I don't understand Gogo, within, out?" Gogo chuckled and held onto Subira.

"You know you carry a blessing to us all, this is the only thing that you should put your attention on, this alone."

"Gogo it is all very well that others are aware of this great change, but I worry for I know somehow there will be loss." Gogo stopped for a moment.

"Ahh, do not worry my Empress, this emotion does not change time but can surely grey your hair" they both laughed and continued walking to the gardens, enjoying the warmth of the yante.

***

Word had not yet reached the palace of Saggitta or the Volker clan, the King was now getting very impatient and sent out more men to see if they could find out anything from the trackers. The Volker Prince Kaydor had now finished dinning with his daughter Sundella, earlier they had completed training of the suns, this technique was only exposed to the older children. His spirit was stirred by the maturity of Skylan's son Ulen, he decided to push his daughter in her training session, this was not a problem for her as she was ambitious like her parents.

"I liked the style of the hue Lari form, it's beautiful father, I feel that I have mastered this already, we are stronger than the Saggittan people."

The Princess brought forth and fanned the nine balls of fire putting them into the alignment formation.

The Prince smiled while cleaning out his teeth with a peffol stick, he had eight wives from different royal families. They were strategically selected from surrounding provinces, as this was a political exchange for governing power and alliance, along with his dashing features his estate housed huge amounts of gold but could not match the Anobi mines.

Along with the wives there were three seers which by tradition were handpicked by the King to guard the Prince. By their land laws the Prince was only permitted to father with one woman, only by death of the birth mother could another woman bare his children.

As they were about to retreat to the altar room to continue training after their evening meal, a message was brought to the Prince. A servant informed Kaydor that the two trackers were able to send imprints of plans from Kargel, but they were also informed that one of the men had been captured, the Saggittan tracker. He was also informed that there was a signed treaty outlining an alliance with Commander Grave and King Skylan. Sundella stood quiet, listening to everything the servant was saying, she held tightly onto her father's hand watching Kaydor's expression change from calmness to rage.

"This was more than an insult, the lies from Skylan," he quietly murmured

"and to think we made peace, but this, this will change."

"I knew Skylan had something to hide, but this?"

The servant quivered watching the fury sweep across Kaydor's face

"about three hibbs ago your highness, we were able to locate a signal from them when they sent the plans, but it was then jammed by a frequency coming from Kargel."

"Continue the tracking, have the Saggittan trackers sent the plans to Skylan?"

"No, your highness, their technology could not span that range, it is primitive to our own"

"good, then send scouts to locate them, get a signal to our men, tell them to kill the trackers upon their return."

"Call my troops, it will soon be time to pay a visit to Skylan, now be gone."

The servant nodded, hastily leaving to send the message. The Prince looked down at his daughter still holding her hand they walked off to the altar room to commence training. He had not enjoyed hearing the news that they had lied to him, declaring war upon them was the only way to repay their gesture.

"It is time to move you my child, I have great work to do"

"where? I don't want to go." Pleaded Sundella.

Kaydor glared at his child then remembered her innocence

"Sundella your training will carry on; you must be ready." Her brow furrowed

"is mother coming?"

"No, she is not Sundella, it is time for you to do your rights of passage, Aqualeena awaits you."

"The water City? its wet!" Kaydor chuckled at her sarcasm

"Yes, that maybe so, Samu will prepare you, you must be the child to change everything" Sundella's eyes rolled around trying to figure out what her father meant by this.

"Ah, do you mean I am the prophecy child?"

"You must be, this is the only reason for the betrayal."

With a big smile the child looked up at her father, for she knew that this time would come, for her to grow from child to woman, but would had not thought it would be this soon. Kaydor thought deeply as they walked, he knew she was the heir to the throne and now he believed that through his tribe the prophecy would be fulfilled. Their ancient scrolls spoke of tales that any one of the children of Kemi could be the keeper of light. One of the scrolls spoke of five warriors becoming one and their kin receiving the holy light, this could be their time to have the honour of having the power of the planet.

Sundella's mind was racing,

"Father, does this mean we are at war with Saggitta? I will protect our people, we are magnificent" Kaydor looked down at his daughter with admiration.

His child was five lucas and spoilt to the core, her father gave her everything and anything that she desired.

Sundella was surrounded by luxury, dozens of maids lay under her command, which this obnoxious child abused with great pleasure. Sundella was a new breed of Volker people, the Prince with his fanatical addiction of vanity had handpicked her mother from thousands of Volker women, she possessed an element of darkness and danger that he desired. Sundella, like her mother was beautiful but shared the same fixed attitude with control, power and superiority.

With a cunning look on her face the young child turned to her father

"father what of the solar ultraviolet flare, I want to learn this."

The Prince looked at his daughter smiling with delight as they continued with her lesson.

"Once you learn the fundamentals my child you will be unstoppable." Sundella smiled at her father's reply and took her stance ready for combat.

***

Lady Cruel had now used all her powers to try and break the trackers tongue, he had revealed no information, he knew that time was not on his side and he could not fight Cruel for much longer. Commander Grave entered the room along with Aja,

"let us see what you can extract from this infiltrator, summon the re-conditioner we can use this beast."

Aja walked towards the man and placed her hands over his forehead closing her eyes she began the sighting. Jealously riddled though Cruel as she watched the priestess, this was not a gift that she possessed but yearned for.

The priestess was able to extract memory imprints from the mind of the tracker, she saw the meeting, the blueprints at the tavern and the drainage system, along with the meeting in Saggitta.

"They came through the drainage system, they possessed maps from Bernal" Her voice echoed as she continued to see.

The more she sighted, the more her voice rebounded around the metal clanged walls, words from her mouth became unclear as she muttered under her breath, she then closed her colourless eyes to reawaken from the sighting.

"So, it was them who had my blueprints, send word to the ground to seal all of the drainage system openings and deploy my foot soldiers."

"Priestess what else did you see?" Aja opened her eyes,

"Commander Grave I can use him for my work to retrieve the Autom scrolls" with a slight pause she quickly answered,

"for you Commander he will be useful."

Lady Cruel gazed deep into Aja's eyes irritated by the way she was influencing her husband's decisions. The priestess stared straight back at Cruel silently informing her that she was not intimidated at all.

"I will lock out his thoughts this will give us control over his will."

"Interesting priestess a unique gift you hold, Duke was right to have you with us." Aja glanced down thinking about her husband's true motives.

The Commander's delight with Aja's skills provoked Cruel even more and she left the room in a temper. The priestess smirked, as she knew she had not given all the information to Grave. Her husband entered the room along with Kabbastian, Aja beckon the boy closer to her then held onto his hand, with her own plan at the forefront of her mind she now schemed to overturn Commander Grave's success of controlling the Autom scrolls.

Her family would be at the nucleus of accomplishing this immense height, she would become the sovereign ruler of Nu Oarren and Kemi. As Commander Grave followed in pursuit of his wife, he paused for a moment to look back at Aja, he did not like this solidarity between the three of them. Aja slowly turned to see him at the door, just staring at her, it was then she realised how she could use both Duke and Grave to her advantage.

Thinking quickly, she seductively batted her green eyes at Grave; smiling a smile only a man of greed and ego filled with a delusion of grandeur would understand the signals she was quietly projecting to him, Grave nodded and closed the door. The priestess chuckled as she looked at her false son staring up at her, she was gaining back some control and now felt invincible, Kabbastian stared at his adopted mother sensing the pleasure she was feeling, her revenge made her worse than Grave and Duke put together. Delighted, Duke turned to her

"you have done well Aja, with this we can change things to our advantage."

"Our advantage?" Kabbastian side eyed his Father, Aja stroked the officer's face smiling,

"oh yes Duke, yes my love.

--- CHAPTER 23 ---

QUEEN ADAMA'S ARRIVAL

The yantes heat fell upon the Islands and their surroundings, Queen Adama, Bakko, Junn and some protectors had now reached the Islands. Murrock along with Nyper and the protectors awaited the party to enter the hut. Empress Subira was resting in her quarters, Gogo appeared smiling as Queen Adama entered the hut. "Queen Adama" Gogo bowed gracefully to greet the Queen,

"the Empress is resting, my Queen." Adama smiled embracing Gogo with a hug. "It's been soo long Moma Gogo since I have been here, I have missed your presence and the peace here."

"We have much to talk about my Queen, do you wish to rest first?"

"No, the journey has kept an anxious knot in the soul, I would prefer to speak Moma Gogo, there is are so many things occurring that I can not rest until my mind is clear."

They both ambled off into Gogo's room, closing the door behind them, as they sat Adama slumped down in the chair distressed; braking down into flood of tears. In a motherly embrace Gogo held onto the Queen, allowing her to release all the pressure of staying strong for her daughter and Javari. Adama sobbed and spoke through her heartbreak.

"Will she live Gogo? This is too much for my child, my grandchild, this is too much to bare." With a gentle tone the old woman responded

"Adama, I cannot answer this my Queen, she is strong, and the child grows well, your wisdom alone has given Subira an opportunity to unfold the closed and open the new, we must pray that the prophecy will reveal its powers."

"What of the leckon bracelet?"

"The Guardians will come, fear not my Queen they chose you, remember that." Adama's response was of a sombre tone,

"Javari is strong, but I am troubled by the burden he bears, the attack on them was just the beginning."

"Our King is a wise ruler and knows more than he reveals, the road ahead hides unknown routes, but we know that this transformation has begun my Queen." Gogo softly patted Adama on her leg to comfort her concern of the future.

They continued to talk for many hibbs until Subira joined them from her afternoon nap, there was a knock at the door by Subira's maid. Subira entered the room tailed gated by little Nyper, she ran up into her bed watching them closely. Gogo glanced at the creature then got up to give Subira her chair.

"I'll leave you; we will talk later."

The old woman departed leaving mother and daughter to be alone. Subira got off the chair and fell into her mother's lap, as she sobbed, Nyper slowly climbed out of her basket bed and settled by the Empress' legs. Adama stroked her daughter's hair then began to sing a sweet lullaby, as her voice resonated around the room, Nyper rocked her head side to side and began to purr along to the comforting melodies.

"I'm so glad that you are here mother, but I long for my husband, I need him." Adama continued singing, holding back her tears.

The sound travelled through the petite cracks around the hinges of the door and drifted into Murrock, Gogo, the hand maidens and protector's ears, everyone became silent as they listened to Adama's classical ancient tongue. Memories overwhelmed them and thoughts of home, safety and love flooded their thoughts, it gave relief for a moment's breath and a glimpse of peace from all that had happened within a few camalas and what was to come.

Both Bakko and Junn were seated at the door to the hut listening along with the others.

"Do you think the prophecy will come to pass? Sonkel doesn't believe, so do you?" Bakko bit into a fruit crunching away, not responding.

"Bakko! You have no answer brother?" He took a big sigh

"I have none, but it will come to pass one way or another."

"We must protect our family at all costs, this is what I am sure about Bakko, the prophecy is secondary to our Kingdom"

Bakko stopped chewing

"you have a small brain Junn, if the prophecy is not fulfilled there will be no Kingdom, no planet and no people"

"So.... we will have to evacuate our planet and go where? Suppose this change that is coming takes out the galaxy?" With raised eyebrows Bakko gazed to the skies rolling his eyes.

"Then...it was nice knowing you brother." Bakko laughed as Junn contemplated his brother's words and grabbed for another piece of fruit.

--- CHAPTER 24 ---

THE VOYAGE

The camalas passed and Aja's influence on Commander Grave grew intensely, they spent a great time repositioning their attack on the Camu hills, her plan was now unfolding, and control was soon in her grasp. Lady Cruel watched over her very closely yante by yante but could not read her movements, the priestess was too intelligent to be caught out now, she had no intention to give such immense power to alien invaders and jeopardize her victory over Nu Oarren and the prophecy.

In the pursuit of power Aja played games with both her husband and Grave and she was delighted as they both tried desperately to state a claim over her. The priestess would call for Grave to meet her in her quarters to discuss the next steps, then summon her husband. He would walk in on them laughing and exchanging gestures of endearment.

Other yantes Aja would be lovingly caressing her husband's face in the presence of Cruel and Grave, this would annoy the Commander because he fed off control, power and attention. Aja used Cruel's jealousy to her advantage, by training Kabbastian and allowing him to play tricks on Cruel as this would infuriate her. The child grew strong with his training from Aja, he learnt quickly, and Aja was impressed with this because he was a different species. Cruel complained that Kabbastian would not listen to her and knew he was plotting with his mother, once she tried to open a door while Kabbastian was next to her and it wouldn't open, as the child saw her about to kick it, he unlocked it making Cruel fly into a table. Arguments would break out with Grave over Aja and her lack of trust towards her, Grave sensed that Cruel was jealous of the time he was spending with the priestess and did his best to reassure her, but she was right to be jealous.

Over the camalas Grave began to warm to Aja even more and at times made advances towards her, Aja knew that this was the time. The priestess was revelling in the fool's naivety and falling into her trap, she was now in control of them both. Cruel tried desperately to do the same to Aja, but the priestess merely left the room every time she saw that Cruel was trying to make her jealous by getting the attention of her husband Duke, Aja was always one step ahead of them.

The timing of her plan was crucial, and she knew this, the royal child would soon be born. With all her books, maps, scrolls and skills, she worked out the time frame when and where. By eliminating any safety locations, she knew of would narrow it down, she sent her new maids and some guards to each district where there were safe spots created for the royal families. The only place now left to explore, was Nu Jahri and by using her maps, seeing and scrolls she was able to plot out the Empress' birthing channel room.

Aja sat in her chambers plotting away to weaken the strong hold of Grave over her husband. Every chance she had she would sooth her husband's ego by implying that Grave was weak and that they would surely kill them both once he had in his possession the Autom scrolls. Yante by yante, camala by camala she wore him down until one night he confided in her how he could prepare an attack on Nu Oarren. Aja using her charm to encourage Duke and they forged a new plan. Only the priestess knew the powers of Nu Oarren and how she could overthrow the King, but not everything had been shared with her through her lucas of training, even the other priestesses and priests including Duke knew not of this protection. King Javari, Foruth, Dacken and the guardians of Aluke knew how to protect their kingdom.

All ashshun she spent time plotting the lari constellation and the appointed time was now; this was the time the scrolls would appear and only then. Aja hurried to her feet and called the guards to her chambers, a message was sent to Commander Grave, that the time to head to the Camu hills was now. They were to leave at the morning dawn to reach there before the next realignment movement, its mystical force field would be at its weakest point and if it was attacked at any other time it would implode, destroying everything. The passageways and decks were filled with slaves, soldiers, servants and troops locking doors preparing for the voyage. A guard hurried through the crowds of people and emerged on the upper deck heading towards Commander

Grave, he puffed and panted as he reached his leader.

"Commander the priestess said it is time," Grave gave a signal to his chief Captain and he prepared the departure from Kargel.

A grey dense steam bellowed into the sky; the sound of the heavy machinery began grinding as the cogs turned setting the ship's engines in motion. The goliath ship dislodged from Kargel and one by one a small fleet trailed behind the father vessel bound for the Camu hills. It would take a two yantes journey to arrive, Grave detested flying and would often fall sick, so sailing was the only option to get there before the window of opportunity closed. Aja stayed within her quarters, giving the order for no one to disturb her. The priestess required deep meditation until they reached the Camu hills. Although she tried to connect to Subira the block was still very dominant over her gift and she could only see part imprints.

As they journeyed through the seas, Cruel tried her best to stay vigilant over Aja's movements, although locked away she planted her guards outside the priestess' door. Kabbastian made himself useful for his mother by annoying Cruel. He opened the door to pass the guards some sweets coated with sleeping drugs. Cruel would check in on the guards and in bewilderment she found them slumped in a heap, Cruel raging at their insubordination, changed the guards. Kabbastian repeated this trick a few times before Cruel caught on to his game. When Cruel returned fuming from what she had discovered, she was confronted by a new set of guards replaced by Aja herself. After several attempts to interrogate the guards Cruel shamefully turned on her heels, gracefully unaware that the enchantment kept them obedient to the priestess' beck and call.

--- CHAPTER 25 ---

VOLKER CLAN

Prince Kaydor's daughter was now safely away from Volker heading to Aqualeena. The Prince and his soldiers had in their possession the bodies of Skylan's men along with the blueprints and information. An attack was being prepared for Saggitta, he didn't take kindly to being doubled crossed or his father and kin being insulted. King Walker was not strong enough to join the attack but gave orders for a full strike to bring down Skylan, he had fought beside him through many battles and this deception had broken his heart, he thought that this was the only way to repay them and honour their name once more.

"They must feel our wrath Kaydor, our tribe do not bow down to lies, we came together as comrades to protect our lands but this, this is war, they plotted against their own kind, using the attack on Nu Oarren as a decoy." Said Walker Although Kaydor's heart was full of revenge he wanted to tackle it different way.

"Father we must strike wisely" warned Kaydor

"wisely? Wisely? Attack now before our walls are filled with Grave's soldiers, Skylan hated that we were stronger than them, they are coming to take our spoil our gold, our birth right, they must know we are the receivers of the light, so they come to destroy us before Sundella reaches womanhood."

"Sundella is gone, she is safe"

"good, then move out our troops and destroy them, destroy their lands, destroy them all!!" demanded the King

"Father shall we consult the seers?"

"Seers! Seers there is no time for this, our time is running out and so is my patience kill... them... all!!"

The King rose up from his throne and stormed across the floor stopping inches from his son's face, his foot men hurried to be by his side in case he toppled to the ground, catching his breath he stood wide eyed at his son

"Your mother died helping to bring peace, no one dare question me, now war, war! We need no evidence!"

Kaydor stared into his father's eyes and could see the lucas of pain locked in every wrinkle of his face, his mother died many lucas ago as part of the fifteenth sisterhood of worshipers from the fold of Aluke, these women all fought desperately to bring back an alliance over Kemi. Something wasn't sitting well with Kaydor's soul, although just like his father's thirstiness for revenge was in his spirit, his intuition was telling him something different, but he bowed cowardly then retreated to descend on Saggitta.

"Assemble my men, we will visit Saggitta once the ashshun has fallen, bring my phantom sword."

The King peered at his son feeling triumphant over his decision

"yes......yes!" As Kaydor marched out of the throne room he twisted his head back just enough for his father to hear.

"I shall honour our bloodline father, soldiers send for my wife, tell her to meet me in our chambers, she will ride out with me!"

Gradually sitting down on his throne King Walker felt fulfilled, as his son marched away, he grew more confident, that this time the prophecy would come to pass and his beloved wife Queen Dia would truly be revenged.

***

There was an unsettling atmosphere throughout the Kingdom of Nu Oarren, when Sonkel had been given news of the movement of Grave and his unorthodox elusive battalion. His spies from Etha had sent word to the Lieutenant that Commander Grave's ships had crossed their boarders, but they were unaware of their final destination. Sonkel summoned for the King to meet at the tetragon combat quarters and relay this new information. Warning alarms and messengers were sent out to neighbouring cities and countries sharing the news of Grave and his location.

"King Javari" he entered the quarters along with Dacken and Fourth

"Sit Sonkel, enlighten us on your findings."

"We know that Grave is advancing towards the Kianda oceans, it seems he is not bound in our direction"

"this does not mean he cannot change his course, the warlords must be deployed, send word to Skylan and Walker we must meet and prepare for war on our Kingdom, it will not be destroyed by the hands of this charlatan and..." Javari looked at Foruth who gently nodded in agreement

"and have you heard any news on the priestess?" Taking a big gulp, Sonkel sipped from a cup

"No, no my King, our men have not been successful in locating her whereabouts, someone is harbouring her"

Javari looked towards the maps on the table,

"have you thought of Grave?" A puzzled look came over Sonkel's face

"Why do you think she would be with him, the last time anyone linked to the priestess was seen was in the land of Gep and this was camalas ago"

"Well we need to be ready for any attack, my wife is drawing near to the birth of our child and I must leave Nu Oarren reassured that we are impenetrable"

"I will do my best Javari" the King gave a sharp glance that met Sonkel's eyes

"then your best must be impenetrable." Sonkel almost responded back but resorted to bowing his head, as his head rose the warlords entered the room ready for Javari's commands.

--- CHAPTER 26 ---

THE SHIFT

A terrible shriek came from the Empress' quarters Subira woke up in a cold sweat, panicking. Murrock, the protectors and Queen Adama dashed into the room. Trying to catch her breath she gestured to say she was alright, Adama sat beside her on the bed

"Subira are you alright? Was it an ashshun-mare?" the leckon bracelet was glowing bright and everyone's eyes focused on her wrist.

Subira watched the gems until the light in them dimmed, looking up at Murrock and the men she signalled to them to leave. Gogo peeped between the cracks of door while it was being closed, observing if the Empress was well.

"I..." a shallow breath came from the Empress as she wiped her brow

"I... saw a woman, she was tall and dressed in white"

"did you see her face?" questioned Adama,

Subira took her time to try and draw from the dream.

"No, I did not see her face, but she was holding a scroll bound with a golden ribbon"

"what made you scream?" her mother asked concerned

"As she untied the ribbon, the planet shook uncontrollably and I saw everyone die.... including me" Adama stared, frightened by Subira's words, almost losing her breath she swallowed to wet her throat

"hmm, not all dreams are bad, let me call for Gogo to see if she can interpret it for you"

"No, please do not mother somehow I need to work this out for myself"

Adama shuffled herself closer to Subira cradling her under her arm, Subira rested her head on her mother's breast while stroking her pregnant stomach.

"I want to see if I can sleep again to connect back into my dream"

"why don't we pray? Or maybe meditate to relax your mind as Aja taught you?"

An anguished breath fell from her mouth.

"I do miss her, she has gone through so much mother, we could have shared such beautiful moments together, both of our children could of..."

"Say no more my love, for this thinking can only lead to unwellness"

"I do hope she is doing well, I cannot believe that she would ever mean me any harm" Adama dare not to tell Subira of what Aja had orchestrated within the Kingdom's walls.

"Do you believe that the woman could be Aja?" Subira considered this for a moment but was uncertain,

"she did not seem to have any white locks upon her head, it would make sense that I would be dreaming of her for subconsciously I worry for her."

"I wonder why the leckon bracelet was glowing"

"I'll get Gogo"

"No, no I will be fine"

"Don't you trust your guide mother anymore? It happens a lot in pregnancy"

"What does?"

"That the pregnant woman takes a dislike to people they may love" "really, how absurd, our hormones and changes" Subira giggled

"no, I love Gogo, I just do not wish for any fussing, I know you will inform her anyway mother, I ask that I receive no answer from her this yante."

"Do you want me to stay? I can lay next to you" Subira smiled,

shaking her head,

"No wonder tradition keeps us apart, to stop her fearful mother."

"Wasn't it you that screamed, you sound just like your husband"

"he has taught me very well" Adama kissed her forehead and left the room giving her a final glance as she closed the door.

Heading straight to Gogo, Adama needed some answers, the old woman was helping the maids prepare breakfast for everyone.

"Gogo can we talk?"

"come ladies leave us, take these to the dining table, I will need your hands" Gogo handed Adama a knife and pointed to the fruit in the bowl. With unnerving speed Adama blurted out what Subira had told her

"She dreamt of a tall woman in white holding a scroll with a..."

"Queen Adama wait, take your time, was the leckon bracelet glowing?"

Her hands stopped peeling the fruit and turned to her.

"Yes, is this part of the prophecy?"

"It seems that everything is part of the prophecy, she is being protected while being given information at the same time"

"I thought it was the priestess in the dream"

Gogo clasped her face pondering the possibility,

"hmm maybe, maybe not but we must eat"

"Is that your answer to everything?" Placing a tray on her head Gogo tottered off leaving the kitchen and heading to the table.

Adama watched her walk through the door,

"Gogo!!" Her fears pushed out a stern yell, which the old woman paid no attention to.

"What is going on? Can you just give me something?"

Gogo threw a peeled munto fruit that squelched as Adama caught it. Giggling to herself Gogo beckoned her to the table, "please sit down my Queen, an empty stomach causes rattling of the brain, we will talk after your food has digested"

Adama chuckled as she shook her head knowing that, no matter what, Gogo could always bring back balance to a troubled mind.

As the hand maids, protectors, Bakko, Junn and Murrock sat at the table they were entertained by Nyper marching around battling with a piece of ban root whilst trying to imitate the crooning of the ulowpillors.

"it's funnnnn"

they all chuckled at the child enjoying herself and not caring about anything, free from the worries she stayed in tune with her mood. Gogo clapped her hands with delight and opened her arms to Nyper to join them.

"We have had word that this Grave man is on the move, it is nowhere near here, but Javari is sending some warlords"

the cheerful atmosphere became heavy with uneasiness. Both Murrock and Junn nodded over to Bakko,

"We should leave this to discuss away from the table General"

An insulted frown trickled over the Bakko's face, "we will do so" he reluctantly agreed, Bakko had never taken to a woman who had such a high ranking around the royal family and after being informed of her behaviour at the dark chambers he acted cautiously towards her.

---CHAPTER 27 ---

THE INVASION

The ashshun had fallen over the peaky cold mountains of Saggitta, Skylan sat with his children reading their favourite stories from their homelands. He paused for a moment unalarmed by the shuddering of the ground, as the realignment drew closer more disturbances were recorded. The children soon refocused on Skylan as they recited pieces from their history book and re-enacted out the famous battles. Laughing, they twirled and spun the swords of light, Mura the eldest of Skylan's children called out battle commands while Ulen rose and posed perfectly in the air. His smile slowly vanished as Mura reminded him of her mother Kian. Ulen floated down peering at his father's saddened face

"Is everything alright father? Did I not do the moves correctly?" He beckoned Mura to sit on his lap and Ulen joined them.

"You have done nothing wrong my love, I just..."

Mura seemed to read his feelings and wrapped her arms around him hugging him tightly. Skylan adored his children and had a deep connection with them, they were his pride and joy.

"Would you marry again?" Ulen waited for his reply and was distracted by another shudder from the ground.

"They are increasing, good job we can fly!"

"Yes Ulen, actually my boy, let us do that, come." Skylan eased them off his knee to stand but Ulen pulled back at his father's arm,

"what about marriage? We don't mind. Mura could do with a female around, other than the warriors" Mura crinkled her lips with a frown

"I'll take kindly to your gesture Ulen and I agree that she does, maybe it is time" Ulen grinned at his sister while she eyeballed him.

"Let us have an ashshun excursion, guards fetch for my armour, I am taking my children out, you both get ready I have seen how you fight let us see if you can fly nearer than me"

"No way father, we can see a little fat under your chin."

"Let me see how you both can fly fully armoured." The guards assembled his armour and the female warriors helped the King to get ready.

"We will take the back route"

"how far will we go?"

"To Nu Jahri?"

"Yes father, that is a good idea, we have not been there for such a long time"

"Mura, Ulen we will see, so let's go." Skylan focused on his energy and formed his wings, his children followed and shot off into the dark skies.

Two guards flew behind them for protection as they soared higher and higher.

"Keep up!"

Skylan flew, in bellows of laughter as his children fought hard to out fly him, they had not flown with their armour before and it was testing the Princess and Prince.

They went to and fro, twisting around and around the noctilucent clouds forming small tunnels. Skylan waved his arms creating balls of light throwing them at the children with glee. As they hovered above their lands, a guard flew urgently to join them.

"My King, the Volker clan are marching on our lands and striking the base of our mountain" Skylan expanded his wings in fury.

"What are you saying? speak up" the altitude was making it difficult to hear the warrior, Skylan pointed to a mountain top and the flew franticly towards it to find out what was happening. As they landed the guard repeated to the King,

"Volker attacks! Walker is attacking our lands!"

"Why?" Ulen blurted out

"That must have been why the ground has been shaking, it was them!!"

Skylan fearfully looked at his children, his son was right. You two take them, they are the chosen ones, take them to Gogo now!! Pointing to one of the guards.

"You follow me" Skylan shot into the air, Ulen wriggled from the arms of the guard and flew after his father

"No, father we will fight with you!" Skylan stopped dead in the air "you will do what I say, take your sister and take this" he quickly pulled from his small finger a ring and pushed into Ulen's hand.

"All will be well but do what I say!" Ulen flung his arms around his father, interlocking his fingers behind his back, the guard tugged and pulled at him as he held on tightly.
A painful yell echoed through the air as Ulen's grip was broken,

"take him, take my children away!!" his children's screams haunted Skylan's ears as they disappeared in the skies.

Skylan descended with haste, making his way to his warriors who were shooting after the Volker men. They were discharging an assortment of weapons including their own powers. Skylan met his warriors at the foot of the mountain, where in the distance he could see Kaydor and his wife mounted on his ground ship. Skylan roared out

"Kaydor! Why do you invade our lands?" Kaydor clasped his hand in tight fist commanding his soldiers to cease.

"You have defiled our treaty and betrayed our lands, for this we bring war to your doors"

Skylan mounted his rider along with his men and flew out towards Kaydor who was being lowered to the ground. The two men were five steps apart, Kaydor was handed some papers and the imprints from Kargel,

"Is this your seal Skylan?" The paper was handed to one of Skylan's men who hurried to show it to his King.

"You attacked our lands without question, you must know that our children..."

"Your children have nothing to do with this, now tell me if this is not your seal! Skylan's warrior opened the scroll revealing a signed document between both Skylan and Commander Grave" Skylan eyes fixed on the seal in horror, his royal seal and his signature.

"I know not of this, this cannot be"

"Is, it, your seal? Raged Kaydor, his veins popping from his neck.

"Is it?" Skylan looked up from the document, bewildered by what was happening,

"yes, it is my seal, my signet ring, someone must of... but this Kaydor is not my doing, why would I forge an alliance with Grave?"

"Are you going to blame the Tau Skylan?" Kaydor's voice lowered as he stared deep into Skylan's eyes.

"Attack" In one swift action, Kaydor drew his phantom sword in the direction of Skylan striking him in the chest, hurling him off his rider. His two warriors grabbed hold of him before he hit the floor. Kaydor struck again this time overpowering his men and slicing Skylan through his breast plate from his chest to face. Warriors swarmed in all directions; blasts bombarded the Saggitta lands, lighting up the ashshun skies. Kaydor retreated to his ship and advanced with his army to finish Skylan. Skylan's men surrounded their King, ready to fight. The four strongest and fastest men grabbed hold of Skylan scooped him up taking him out of the battle.

"No... I did not do this to us... Let me fight with my men" A helpless cry fell from the wounded King as he was dragged away from the battle.

Kaydor relaunched his phantom sword tossing it into the air just missing the feet of one of the warriors. Although Kaydor wanted to honour his father, his conscience was playing on him, he saw the pain of his father's face, but allowed Skylan to get away

"Take it all down, destroy their palace and their weapons."

The Volker tribe were unaware of the new strain of power that the Saggittan warriors had being harbouring, now that the King was safe, they unleashed their ora light. It was forbidden to be used after the treaty with King Javari had been signed but they had no choice. A blue electric outer body shield formed around each man and woman and the attack soon became one sided. Kaydor's soldiers could not fight against this power, they began to retreat from the force that had been unleashed upon them. The angry Prince Kaydor watched as the palace pillars toppled down the mountain causing an avalanche of rocks, that was enough for him and he signalled his soldiers to move out, his wife could see that her Prince was defeated, not by King Skylan but by living in the shadow of his father.

***

Aja meditated for many hibbs, all her probing and scouting had confirmed that Nu Jahri was harbouring the Empress. Kabbastian had finished practising with the alignment of fake scrolls, he was able to use his mind to turn them in the air and disintegrating them to dust with his breath. The priestess had injected her son with crafted solutions to unlock his DNA and bring forth greater powers. He was kept away from the other children to keep his mind pure for task ahead, the priestess requested that even Duke should not interact with their son for his polluted mind could affect his transformation. They were at least eighteen hibbs away from landing at the shores of Rakbea, after that they would have to fly to Camu. Commander Grave was in his quarters being attended to by his Tau slaves, they massaged his stiff arthritic shoulders soaking them with oils provided by the priestess. Lady Cruel watched them cautiously as they groomed her husband, she beckoned one to do her feet. The slave's fought back tears from the oder of her sweaty boots.

"You will make them sick my love, we need them" Grave chuckled to himself as his wife's side-eyed him.

"We must be focused, the best way to be ready is this"

"you are vain"

"but you love me for it" Cruel relaxed into the chair as the massaging hands of the slave soothed her smelly, aching toes.

"Are you sure I cannot go visit the priestess I need to see what she is doing or plotting"

"My lady, let her do what she needs to do, we will soon have in our possession the scrolls and what we have been dreaming of"

Cruel's thoughts left their quest for a tali and fretted,

"do you think they will find us?" Grave batted the slave's hands away and propped himself up on his elbows,

"how long have we been here? How many lucas, we have crossed galaxies and yet there has been no sign of any of them, enjoy your foot rub and be excited about the fruits of our labour" he sunk back down summoning the women back. As they enjoyed this moment together on sector five Duke was planning his attack, Aja had given him new co-ordinates to enter Nu Oarren and destroy their artillery. He followed the maps, meridian lines and plotted the practise points to lay explosives and take down his once loved kingdom. Although having his wife beside him, he now desired complete power over the scrolls and would do anything to have them in his hands. When they were youngsters; Javari had spent time pondering over the forces of the scrolls and if they could get their hands on them, they could make their planet heal, the King had always confided in Duke more than any of his cousins. The Imperial Officer understood how painful his betrayal was to his loyal friend. He mused over the past of what could have been but was soon brought back to reality by noticing the Tau province circled on the map, why did the priestess pinpoint their lands? He needed to ask her, but he knew better than to disturb her while she meditated

--- CHAPTER 28 ---

THE TWO KINGS

Gogo was seated at the round table in her room with seven other spiritual sisters, they had just finished fasting and praying when a maid knocked on the door.

"Momma Gogo our defence soldiers have located Saggittan warriors trying to get into our lands, the protectors have joined them along with Bakko and Junn."

All the elders stood quickly, waiting for Gogo's instruction.

"Let us go to them, something is wrong, we have seen some symbols dying."

The old woman toddled off followed by the elders, Murrock stayed behind to be near Subira as she rested through the sweltering yante. The water defences were lowered; allowing the warriors to fly in unscathed. They landed, exhausted but safe with the children sleeping in their arms, maids hurried to take the children to the hut, but first brought forth healers to check them over.

The warriors told General Bakko and Officer Junn of the attack on their lands and warned that the Prince of the Volker clan was on a rampage to kill their King.

"We must send word to Sonkel and warn him that the defences must be increased around Nu Oarren, Junn go send a message."

Junn glared at his brother as he ordered him like a child, turning on his heels he headed off along the bridge with some of the warriors, passing Gogo and the elders to send the signal. Hearing of the awful devastation across the Saggitan's land, the elders wept and mourned for those who had lost their lives defending their homelands.

"You must go to Volker and confront the King, take some guards, he must understand that this was an unfaithful and unjust act of ego, the dead must be buried together, it must be so."
Gogo wiped away the tears for she knew this was only the beginning, comforting two of the sisters they left to have council with King Walker.

"Keep all this news from the Empress and Queen Adama, they need not worry, inform Murrock, but the children must be kept sedated and sent to..." Gogo paused for moment, Bakko stood waiting for her to finish her instructions but ceased speaking and focused on the elders

"My sisters will take care of this." Two other elders stared deeply into Gogo's eyes bowed and walked off in the direction of the children.

***

Skylan was resting safely in his chambers, with guards positioned outside and around the corridors. He had been attended to by the King's medics who had repaired his wounds as best they could, however he was now branded with a horrible thin lined scar up the right side of his face. His warriors had managed to fly the great distance to get him into Nu Oarren and to the medics. They had received no word from warriors they left, the state of Saggitta, or from Walker regarding the attack; no one was certain if anyone was alive and if the mountains were still standing. Javari had given orders to Lieutenant Sonkel to dispatch a fleet of warlords to Saggitta. The King needed answers, his intuition was telling him that, even though Skylan's sedated explanation was confirmed by his men, he knew something deeper was at large.

"Send for a seer, the purer the better" Dacken left to bring back a child. Skylan summoned his men to prop him up.

"I do not believe in seers, I am telling you Javari that I had nothing to do with this, it's a forgery!" Javari lowered himself slowly into his chair

"Then if it is a forgery, you will not mind the seer, was it your ring? Was it your signature?" Shamefully he hung his head, but his blood was boiling with rage.

"Why would I do this to my people? Kaydor attacked my lands for no reason, none!" The King tilted his head in questioning and repeated it again

"Was it your signet ring? Was it your signature?" Skylan drew strength from his pain and bellowed the echo bouncing around the walls of the chamber

"We are getting nowhere Javari! This is Walker's doing, we have been a threat to them ever since the last war!" Javari paused for a moment before replying calmly, "ever since you took the gem from the fold of Aluke?" Skylan's nostrils flared, he knew he was guilty of that but refrained himself from answering.

At that moment Dacken entered accompanied by a small Gep girl,

"Come to me my little one, I ask that you seek out some answers for me, it seems we have some missing pieces that will clear up a puzzle"

Her little face quivered with fright, holding her hand to reassure her, Javari led her to Skylan.

"Why use a child Javari?"

"Children are innocent, she will see clearer than older seers and it is imperative we have an uninfluenced vision in this case, come child."

Her little eyes opened wide as she attempted to find her voice; desperately trying to avoid looking at the newly scared King,

"your highness, I am not strong enough to hold his hand yet, I need to hold his head." Javari smiled at her, thinking of his own child that would soon be born.

"Then do so my child," her hands shook as she placed them onto his temples

"What is it you are seeking your Highness?"

"King Skylan says he was falsely accused of signing a treaty, tell me what you see little one." A confused look spread across her face,

"Your highness, what is a treaty?" Javari gave a sympathetic sigh

"A scroll little one, that has his name on it and has someone else's too, it shows that they agree about something."

Her little brain understood the King's words, her eyes closed, the room went silent with everyone fixed on the small girl. Her eyes could be seen moving at speed under her eyelids, almost as quickly as they had started, they stopped.

"You signed the scroll.... the... treaty, but your hand was lifted to seal the wax" Skylan's mouth opened releasing a startled intake of breath, as Javari did not mention the seal the child was seeing the truth,

"No, this cannot be true" Skylan gasped

"Be quiet Skylan, don't interrupt her" Javari quickly brought the attention back to what she was sighting. Her mouth started to open again,

"Ahhhh.... tavern in.... Bern...Bernal, you sit with your men, a pretty, pretty lady, with purple hair, you're dancing and drinking from golden... goblets, you're laughing, you look at her but I see from the reflection of another goblet she pours clear water into your drink." Skylan's eyes opened wide and stared across at Javari.

"Purple hair lady takes you away, your men are laughing and drinking, she is dancing, you are speaking strange" the girl continued.

They all stared at Skylan,

"you don't sound well at all, your words sound like you are falling asleep, the drink sinking into your blood, I can feel your breath weaken, my head hurts, she asks you to sign something, you laugh while shaking your head and sign slowly, I see the name Co....mman.....der, she moves your hand and presses it in wax then puts it on the scroll, your eyes are dizzy, you shake, ahhhhhh.....you sleep." Javari gently held the child,

"Very good my child, we ask you to come back now, come back"

As her eyes opened her body became limp, Dacken took over from the King and lifted her from the floor and carried her carefully out of the room.

Everyone felt the shock and embarrassment seeping from King Skylan, he was now having a blurred account of visiting Bernal about one and half lucas ago and recalling a moment talking with a purple haired woman but nothing else.

"Oh no! What have... I... done" he tried to catch his breath, holding this hand tightly to his chest,

"what have I done? I have betrayed the Saggittan's, Javari am I to blame? I signed death on my Kingdom" trying not to collapse he sniffed; taking shallow breaths through his words

"what... else...did. I do?" Javari saddened by the truth sat back in his chair contemplating all that was said.

Forgetting his-self for a tali, Javari gave a sarcastic reply

"Well, we could bring the seer back" All eyes swivelled to the King, Javari released his words were not a noble response but full of ego, for he was angry at Skylan's foolish weakness resulting in death.

"Please forgive me for that King Skylan"
Gripping his weary head Skylan sobbed for disgracing his family and bringing death upon his lands, he could not lift his face to Javari nor to his men. Javari pondered over the truth and this time waited for a moment to speak,

"We need to pay a visit to King Walker, yes your miscalculation of trust put the sweetest of the wonder oil in your eyes and you did not keep your guards active, it is a terrible, terrible price to pay."

Skylan listened while tears rolled silently down his cheeks, his men also fighting back tears of their own, stood straight to hold their dignity for their King.

"Leave us! All of you. Dacken, Foruth you too."

Javari knew the pain Skylan was feeling so well and was humbled as laying heavy on his chest was a reminder of Duke, what he had done by hiding the truth about the Tau province. As the door closed behind the men, King Javari stood up, walked over to Skylan and hugged him, Skylan looked up for a moment catching Javari's eye and broke down; crying on the floor. Javari held him;

allowing him to be consumed by his emotions and tears. Beyond the door everyone flinched at the mournful screams, with hast Dacken and Foruth opened the door, they would disobey the King if it meant saving his life. Javari nodded to them and they closed the door again. Through his tears Skylan tried to speak,

"Javari, how could I have been so stupid..."

"My friend, to lose your wife Kian at such a young age and needing the attention of love, that was not stupid, it was not guarding yourself that was, we all as Kings have made mistakes."
Skylan's temper started to rear its ugly head

"Walker, Walker did not even try to find out the truth, he stills holds in his heart his wife's death that I was to blame, they used this to..."
Javari quickly stopped him.

"We all lost parents and loved ones that luca! Skylan would you have requested council with Walker, would you even if he were pleading with you, would you?"
The silence that followed answered Javari's question,

"you would have done the same thing, betrayal if not harnessed can be deadlier than the first act." Skylan could not lie

"you are right, in my own ignorance I would have done the same"

As both Kings sat on the floor crippled by the ordeal, Javari's thoughts went to his children

"Where are Mura and Ulen?" Through a sniff Skylan wiped his tears

"Nu Jahri, I... sent them to Gogo"

An uncomfortable silence fell in the room as Javari thought about the safety of his wife and child.

"Gogo will keep my prophecy children safe, I must tell them that I am alright."

Javari side eyed his words, 'prophecy children' he thought,

"that is why they attacked my lands; they must know that..."

"No!"

"No Javari?"

Javari continued

"No, not yet, I will let my men send a coded message, but it is too soon, we are not sure what else you have revealed, my friend."

Skylan lifted his head looking straight at Javari.

"Then bring an older seer, as I don't want to hurt that child's mind." With a faint smile Javari nodded in agreement,

"once we have contacted Walker both you and I will pay their Kingdom a visit, there are more enemies at large and we do not know what else this Commander Grave has up his sleeves.

--- CHAPTER 29 ---

THE LECKON BRACELET

Subira awoke suddenly in a cold sweat, a maid rushed over to her

"What is it my Empress?"

"I don't know, but my bracelet is blazing like fire, I could feel it, look how it is glowing"

The leckon bracelet was pulsing like a heartbeat, they could almost hear a tone

"Did you hear that?" The maid nodded frightfully,

"call for Gogo," she hurried out of the room to find Gogo.

Murrock was seated outside the room worrying about the King and the news about Skylan but she was still haunted by Lani-ma's death.

"Is the Empress alright?"

"Captain Murrock, the Empress' leckon bracelet woke her from a dream, it glows like fire"

Murrock was unsure for the Empress' safety and swiftly entered the room.

"My Empress"

"Murrock look, I think something bad has happened, is everything alright with the King?" Murrock was about to answer her when Gogo opened the door.

"Let me see" she toddled over to the bed

"Murrock you did not answer me."

She peered over to Gogo for some help, as she did not wish to lie to the Empress.

"Look how it is glowing, does it hurt you?"

"Ah no, no but in my dream, it was burning like fire, is everything alright?"

Gogo drew up a stool and sat close to Subira who was now sitting up straight to hear what she had to say.

"Do you know how to meditate Empress Subira?"

Subira was not fooled by her feeble distraction, she now knew that something had happened.

"I have had lucas of lies, things kept from my ears Gogo, if there is something wrong please tell me the truth"

"Do you meditate?" Gogo repeated, not even blinking

"Gogo!" Subira's temper started to rise

"Gogo Amakia!"

"Empress I do not ask to dishonour you but to remind you, that you must regain your calm and the leckon bracelet will stop glowing."

Her mind was fixed on her unanswered questions, she had forgotten about the bracelet.

"Be calm my Empress, take yourself to the amethyst chambers, please close your eyes."

"I prefer the black tourmaline chambers; the old woman smiled at the Empress' high-spirited answer.

"Gogo I know you mean well and I need to be calm but I have a gut feeling, I just need some answers"

"Stressing will only make you unwell Empress, once you are still we shall discuss what is upon us, now please, join me."

The pleading voice of Gogo soothed Subira's questioning,

"Alright, alright Moma, take me there...... but tell me the truth."

Gogo rested her hands on her lap as they both closed their eyes to focus.

***

Junn had just returned to share the report back from Sonkel,

"Javari is on his way to Volker, that stupid Skylan had been drugged by some woman under Commander Grave control and his tribe was attacked because of this control, hence mountain's blowing up"

"What is this you are telling me? We should have never left Nu Oarren! Sonkel can't lead my army" Junn frowned at Bakko's arrogance

"Your army? really Bakko? Sonkel may not be a general but I am sure that our brother can take care of our Kingdom while we are away"

"are you taking sides now brother?" Junn walked over to the end of a bridge as the salty breeze rushed up from the shore, he looked down to the sea, the ulowpillors calmly crooning as they swam playfully, close to the land. Bakko grabbed his brother and childishly pretended to throw him off the bridge, the hemp rope wobbled and stretched under his body weight.

"Are you crazy Bakko? Really?"

"We are twins, if I die you die, I wouldn't have let you go juvenile" Bakko laughed as he pulled him back.

"You take things too far sometimes Bakko, this is no time to joke around! Enough brother, enough!" Bakko continued laughing and pushing his brother.

"You were scared weren't you young one?" Junn boxed his hand away while pushing him backwards until he stumbled.

"Why do you continue to mock me Bakko? I'm soo sick of your childish ways with me, you order me around with little respect in front of everyone, all the time" Bakko's face fell as he saw his brother's irritation.

"It sounds like..."

"It sounds like what? like what?"

"That... you have things bottled up, if I." Junn cut his brother off before he could finish

"Bakko... not now I don't need a bonding session, not here and not from you, not now"

"counselling... per...haps?" Junn smirked at his brother's shabby attempt to lighten the mood.

"Let's be serious Bakko, our family must be protected, Subira needs us around, besides he has Dacken and Foruth by his side, Javari will be well"

"Junn they are not his blood; it is our honour and duty to keep him safe" Junn shook his head

"so... do they,"

"Wouldn't it be better to bring us back together?"

They both fell silent as Queen Adama came strolling towards them carrying Nyper with some of the villager's children tailing closely behind.

"Queen Adama"

"Bakko, Junn, I see you are taking in the sights of this land, I am taking Nyper and the other children over by a gazebo to read them a story, you can join us if you choose" They both chuckled as Junn glanced at his brother

"Queen Adama, I think it would do wonders for Bakko" Adama continued her journey; beckoning them to follow. The children grabbed at Bakko's arms and gave him little choice but to follow; chuckling at the innocence and energy they had, he stuck his tongue out at Junn. The officer was really worried for his cousin's life and although they had to protect the heir to the throne he wanted to be by Javari's side. As he watched their silhouette's disappearing into the horizon, Junn decided to return to the Saggitta warriors to ask them more questions.

---Chapter 30 ---

The Misunderstanding

King Walker lavished in the grasp of victory, in the main great hall of the palace where all his soldiers had assembled ready for this untimely meeting. His son Kaydor had been given news that King Javari, King Skylan and two sisters of Nu Jahri were requesting a presence with the King.

"Do you believe what Javari said is true?" Kaydor asked his father.

"Falsehood! I thought you killed Skylan boy?" Kaydor seated next to his father scowled at his response.

The trumpet announced the arrival of the Kings, all the soldiers aimed their hands towards them as they walked in with their men. Foruth and Dacken stood either side of Javari as they moved further down the green woven carpet. Unrepentant for the attack Walker was enraged that Skylan was still alive.

"You dare to bring him here on our land, you should be dead with the rocks at the foot of your mountain"

"King Walker, may I first ask for your mercy on this man King Skylan, he was not the cause of this but.."

"King Javari you are a wise man, but this council is on shaky ground"

"May I..."

"No, you may not speak!" Walker's temper was brewing, and Javari quickly quietened King Skylan and continued

"King Javari, state your plea!"

"I have had time to find the truth, my seer has revealed this, I ask that you bring your seers to confirm this"

"How do I know that you all have not added an imprint to come and..." Javari interrupted Walker for he knew what he was going to say.

"King Walker why would I do this? I, we come in peace, only peace, we need each other more than ever" Walker glared at Javari and Skylan and took a deep breath.

"Kaydor send for a seer, in fact bring all of them, soldiers hold your positions." Javari Skylan, Dacken and Foruth watched as Walker's soldiers' hands started to glow. As the women entered the room Kaylor's mind was racing as he noticed Skylan's scar. Five women surrounded Skylan and guided him to sit, they held on to him and repeated exactly what the young Gep child had said. The hall went quiet as the truth spilled out from the seers. Kaydor quickly got to his feet, whispering and realising his actions could have been sustained,

"I told you to get seers" Walker looked up at his son, ashamed of what he had sanctioned. The trumpets blew again, and the two sisters entered the room; walking towards the Kings. They slowly bowed as the crowd waited to hear what they had come to say

"King Walker, thank you for granting us to enter your Kingdom at short notice" with his palms out Walker nodded gesturing them to proceed

"we come with word from Sister Moma Gogo Amakia, about what has taken place this ashshun it has soiled the land and broken a line, a line that our planet needed to breathe, you have killed from pain and brought more pain to others, for this reason you all must be cleansed." All eyes rested on Walker as the sisters continued to speak, pointing to Skylan one of the sister's proceeded

"this yante your soldiers must accompany his men and bury the dead, this must be done by the ashshun moons shine, we will come to see what we can do to help the ground to be still, for you have awoken the fire beneath and disturbed the flow of the prophecy." The hall fell silent with her words, they had all felt the shift of the planet. Walker got to his feet to answer them but was stopped by his son,

"We will honour this sisters, for it was I that carried out this command" Kaydor stepped down the three large steps from the throne and at a steady pace he dismissed the seers and stood before Skylan.

Skylan's warriors helped him to his feet, they stood face to face with memories from the battlefield still fresh in their minds.

"Your men brought forth a weapon that is forbidden"

"Yours brought death and I bare the scares not just on my face but in my heart, I do not know what I will return to, you are fortunate my children are safe and well."

Kaydor raised his eyebrows, ready to attack again but the two men looked deep within each other's souls that were full of anger, shame and vengeance. The sisters placed their hands on both men to calm them down.

"You can war inside your bodies but outside we all pay, King Walker we will return in three yantes after the burial to deal with your heart, may the past rest in peace!" Kaydor glanced back at his father as he understood what the sisters were saying, slowly reaching out his right hand he waited for Skylan to shake it. It took a tali but Skylan glanced at his men who nodded in agreement and shook his hand. From a bowed head, Walker got up from his throne and ambled over to Javari, he signalled to his soldiers to lower their hands.

"The damage has been done my friend, I cannot change what has been done but you have my word King Javari, that I will not ever act in reaction but response" Javari clasped Walker's forearms as comrades,

"had I listened to Prince Kaydor, we would not be mourning our men or his, my grandchildren cannot grow with a bitter grandfather anymore" Walker nodded towards his son

"Nor my son, sisters I await your healing" Kaydor looked at his father surprised at his reply while bowing to his words.

"We must protect our lands together for within our lucas our prophecy shall be fulfilled," Javari looked over at Foruth as he finished his words the ground simultaneously tremored. Their heads turned towards the sisters as they all were astonished at the synchronized moment. Walker's face was stunned

"don't bring the children back until this done" Kaydor's eyes open wide

"but father the texts say ten lucas, Sundella cannot be away from me for so long, this is what you ask..."

"She must live Kaydor, what would you prefer?"

Kaydor's heart sunk, he looked over to his wife who was fighting back the emotions; mirroring his thoughts exactly. Javari listened pondering whether to speak

"our scrolls... predicted eighteen lucas."

"Then it is eighteen lucas, we will not be driven from our planet by anyone or anything, the prophecy shall come to pass this time.." Both Javari and Walker fixed their eyes on Skylan.

"It is not just our planet my Kings it is the universe that is at stake"

The three Kings, Prince and sisters all stood in silence, all considering what lay in store for their bloodlines, Kingdom and now all planets.

--- CHAPTER 31 ---

THE ATTACK AND DESTRUCTION

Within one hibb, they docked near the shores of Rakbea bound for the Camu hills. They could see from a distance the small water fall that marked the joining of the Rakbea mouth opening and its sister sea, some scouts flew ahead of the convoy as ordered, under Aja's guidance they were able to navigate without being seen. Grave and Cruel stood at the shore taking in the beautiful horizon, as they watched the animals scurrying around, blissfully unaware of the invaders, their thoughts were fixed on the scrolls and the power that awaited them. To Grave's deep dislike they boarded the craft, he popped some motion sickness sweets in his mouth given to him by the priestess, Aja followed closely behind them with Kabbastian holding her hand while her guards carried a container and her scrolls.

"Where is Duke?" Cruel asked Aja who was surveying the lands as they flew higher into the skies.

"He is on his way to Nu Oarren" Cruel grunted at the priestess

"What do you me he has gone to Nu Oarren? I told you she was planning something!" Grave, shocked at the news,

"priestess what is the meaning of this? you sent Duke without my say, what for?" Aja uninterested in their display lifted Kabbastian up and propped him on top of the flight panels for him to look out of the window.

"Aja!" She smirked to herself while she could feel their impatience brewing.

"He needs to attack when we do, it will weaken the energy of Camu hills," Grave stood silently, annoyed that she had not revealed this to him.

"Why did you keep this from me? I am the Commander of this invasion, what else are you keeping Aja?" Turning around to face them the priestess smiled through her words.

"Commander... I did not dishonour your leadership, I clearly prepared for your strike to be a success, you did not need to know because, like a faithful servant I am at your bidding, I took the initiative to surprise you with this gift"

"A gift, a gift this is no prize for my husband priestess, you a taking the"

"Cruel!" Grave interrupted abruptly to quieten his wife

"I am vexed by your insubordination, but if what you are saying is correct, then I will consider your gift, but make sure priestess that you tell me everything from now on, I don't need any more surprises" Aja bowed her head playfully at Grave while Cruel scowled at her. As they soared off towards Camu Grave began to doubt the movements of Aja and was starting to believe Cruel's uncertainty.

***

Gogo received news that her sisters were with the soldiers burying the dead, she had noticed that the skies seemed darker than most sunny yantes. Alongside the other elders Queen Adama sat as they prepared a praying ceremony. Gogo stood up and walked over to a large box containing pink quartz crystals. Each elder took a stone and described what they could see, resting them upon the table they spread them around the other stones. Queen Adama quietly observed as they all closed their eyes into prayer meditation. Each stone slowly rose from the table and hovered inches from their resting place. Adama watched as they created layers upon layers until she could almost see a pattern forming, she started to recognize its shapes, it was creating a geometry symbol that she had seen before but could not remember where. Her mind raced to and fro trying to pinpoint their meeting, then her thoughts fixed on the fold of Aluke, it was there with the fifteenth sisterhood of worshippers, the metallic cube shape was planted in the sands with fire opal. Adama remembered them pushing the stones into the ground, but in her memory, she was not seeing herself as an adult but when she was young.

She uttered under her breath "impossible" her only recalling of being at the fold of Aluke was when both her and her new husband had stumbled on the battle.

Adama cautiously watched the elders as more memories started to flood into her mind, her eyes noticed that each layer represented each province, city and country of Kemi, but why? Gogo lifted her hands and the other women followed her lead until they were all clasped together. The stones rotated slowly in the air; a faint light could be seen from each elder's forehead. Adama felt a slight headache as her own forehead began pulsing, she found it difficult to move her head, she felt frozen and locked in time, she was scared of the feeling but kept as still as she did not want to disturb what was happening to her or them.

Beyond the door the Empress sat quietly reading when her focus was distracted by little Nyper, her eyes were wide enchanted by the now glowing leckon bracelet. Murrock notice the creature and tried to break her attention by throwing tiny pieces of ban root at her but this didn't work. The warrior crept closer to her then grabbing her and throwing her over her shoulders she carried her away from the Empress, the wriggling child struggled to break free as she stretched her neck to look back at the bracelet.

Subira had now placed her book down and started rubbing the bracelet feeling its now cool temperature. Her fingers counted over the nine jade emeralds.

"I wonder why there are nine, it's cold too, Murrock, where is Gogo?"

Murrock was busy play fighting with Nyper as she was trying to get back to the Empress and did not hear her. A maid overheard her question

"Empress Subira, they are in her quarters, but they cannot be disturbed your highness as they are praying" Subira nodded

"have you seen my mother?"

"Queen Adama is with them"

"thank you" the maid bowed as she continued about her yantes duties, as Subira continued to rub the stones each one glistened by her gentle touch, her eyes glanced up for a moment as she giggled under her breath watching Nyper trying to wrestle her mother.

The faint echo of the elders chanting prayers brought an eerie calm around the waters. Bakko and Junn were not far from the hut smoking a keba pipe discussing their next plan of action, the sweltering afternoon's heat was draining and rejuvenating their brown skin at the same time. Shaded from the sun the Saggitta soldiers were seated beside them ready to return to their lands. They had all been given news of the meeting at Volker, Skylan sent a request through Javari's men and ordered his soldiers not to bring back the royal children.

***

The lights shone brightly over the province as the evening began to fall, the inhabitants rested unaware of the invasion at hand. Within the quarters and tunnels the anointed followers hurried around moving in and out of chambers collecting the scrolls. Near the upper temple stood a dense black door that was bound with heavy locks and chains, three high priests had in their possession a cluster of keys. Each one of them hurried with their keys to open the padlocks, they pushed the keys into each lock, but the locks would not open. As they attempted to open them again the locks sealed themselves before their eyes, someone had cast a holding spell over the door, the priests were in shock and one of the young apprentices was sent to alert the other high priests and priestess' in the upper chambers. The guardians had now returned to the upper temple to move the high priestess' and priest's, all were present but were now dressed in grey heavy robes. priestess Wallak stepped forward and bowed before them.

"It is time, one camala, the prophecy begins."

Each priest and priestess had in their hand a series of scrolls; they all placed the scrolls on the floor near the guardians. As the scrolls rolled towards the guardians one of them stopped dead, one of the guardians hovered their hand over the scroll.

"This forbidden scroll has been tampered with." Knocking frantically at the door the young apprentice ran in to inform them that the locks on the door could not be opened. Suddenly there was a large blast; the temple shuddered from the immense power of the explosion.

"Is this the shift?" asked Wallak nervously

"No! Wallak, it is not. We must leave" answered one of the guardians

"What about the true scrolls, who tampered with them?"

The guardians looked at each other confused then glanced at one of the priests who had stepped back from the group and hastily left the room,

"leave him!" Wallak was mystified by their answer.

"Guardians, the chambers contain..." The guardians stepped back,

"we must leave them now, call the others for the sacred hill is under attack."

Wallak, the priests and priestesses were astonished by how they were so calm at leaving the scrolls behind but obeyed their demands. The refugees and followers poured out of their tents in panic, another tremendous blast went off, booming in the air, its dust clouds and roaring sound ricocheting off the other mountains; deafening everyone around. Huge boulders plummeted from the mountain tops as people ran frantically in all directions to get away from the debris.

Aja had given the instructions for divers to descend into the river surrounding the hill, they were given co-ordinates to emerge under the middle cavern once Aja broke the seal and received word from Duke. This luca and yante was the weakest time and the weakest part of the hills were the base, its energy dropped so low it was vulnerable as this was a sacred time for followers which Aja knew and used to her advantage. Once the divers were in place, they set more explosives under the lower sacred chambers and waited for the signal to trigger them, the priestess had reached the entrance trailing behind her were Kabbastian, Grave, Cruel and the guards.

***

West of the Camu hills the Imperial Officer Duke was waiting to receive the signal from Aja's men. His troops arrived at the outskirts of Nu Oarren, scouts were sent ahead to fly near the main settlement of the Kingdom, some were dressed in ordinary merchant attire they tried to blend in to gain access through the main gates of the city. There was a lot of activity around the Kingdom's walls, clusters of protectors patrolled,

Nu Oarren was in lock down, everyone was being questioned and asked to produce trading passes. Duke and the soldiers were dressed in Saggitta combat armour redesigned to carry their weapons; they were waiting for the signal to fly over the walls once the defence shield had been disabled. Duke knew the codes would have been changed that morning, so he reverted to old methods to get in the palace, scrapping his initial plan. Duke noticed a large group of Saggitta soldiers entering the gates, he was puzzled by such a large number of their army but quickly blended into their group, fortune was on their side at last. The soldiers found the defence shield gate and shut it down, they hurried to join the rest of the party. Duke signalled to his men to cover their armour but leave the emblem showing and the walk through the gates unnoticed. Once inside they found a quiet place to signal Aja they were in position and ready, there crafts were cloaked and lay far enough away to not be detected. One of the Saggittan soldiers noticed the group but before he could raise the alarm, Duke and his men disbursed into the crowds of people and disappeared out of sight. The officer was familiar with the layout of the streets and meandered through the crowds until they got close to the main transparent gate entrance of the palace. He made the final call and waited to hear from Aja.

***

The purity of her sisterhood vowels were now gone, Aja defiled her bond by muttering a single command on herself,

"the circle of intent, the circle of problems, the circle of the vision of truth" her eyes went white and the circles moved around her face. The lower entrance was now weak enough to allow anyone to walk through its opening. Her hands felt the grey rocks and mould, she closed her eyes

"Now!"

Her voice bellowed to the soldiers and Duke to strike, a monstrous bellowing of explosions went off; shaking the ground and flinging them off their feet. Scrambling up and dusting themselves off, they followed Aja as she marched further into the hill. Some of the scouts mounted their fliers and worked their way up to the highest point of the mountain; destroying each sacred point mapped out by the priestess. The mountain needed to be weakened further for the contents of the scrolls to be revealed. As they arrived at the upper temple they hovered past an opening and glimpsed the guardians, priests and priestess' looking at each other, within a tali all the figures started disappearing along with the scrolls which they noticed on the floor. One of the figures waved their hands creating a swirl of bright yellow gas, its denseness surrounded the room, hiding all from view.

The soldiers attempted to shoot after them through the cloaked vile of smoke, but the figures faded into the air, one of the soldiers hovered closer to look, he shone a light to try and glimpse if they were still there. He was about to step off the flyer to enter through the opening of the stone arch to investigate further, when the upper temple imploded just missing him. The sound trembled and ricocheted waves through the sky, a surge of electrical current flashed from the temple, it was so strong that it short circuited some of the scout's flyers; toppling them to their death. The sound of the upper temple falling resonated throughout the hill. Aja and her assembly were now facing the locked black door, bodies of young priests left behind lay dead along the corridors after they were greeted by the foot soldiers. Aja noticed one of the dead was the faithful friend who had helped her to gain entrance to the scrolls.

The priestess once again closed her eyes and moved her hand across the locks, Commander Grave rubbed his hands together with delight at the thought of possessing the Autom scrolls. As the locks disappeared and fell to the floor, her eyes returned to green, she held out her arms, parting them wide and the doors swung open, the ground shuddered as they walked hastily through the doors. Laying before them were thousands upon thousands of scrolls, the shelves were so heavily crammed that scrolls dangled like leaves.

"How are you going to find the scroll before we all perish?"
Grave commanded as he held Aja by her wrists staring deep into her eyes. Her eyes flitted to her son

"Come, come child" the priestess beckoned Kabbastian to come forward, she bent down and whispered into his ear.
He quickly scampered around the chambers, pulling out scrolls left and right, then as quickly as

he has started, he stopped. The hill shook again, this time more violently.

"Be quick my son" Aja warned gesturing to Kabbastian

"this better not be some trick priestess" cautioned Cruel walking beside her, letting her know she was not trusting her at all.

The child ran along humming to himself for a couple of talis then stopped and pointed. Grave pushed past everyone to seize the scroll.

"No, no hands of blood can touch any scroll first within these walls" stated Aja.

The child pulled out one, two, then three, he held them close to his chest walking back to his mother.

"Open them" as he opened each scroll, they locked together to create one larger scroll.

"Hurry" the hill tremored again; Aja knelt guiding Kabbastian to put the large scroll on the floor.

They all watched in amazement as the scrolls turned to water, then fire, then ice and then finally dust.

"Quickly, quickly child, do as I have taught you."

Kabbastian took from his pocket a small plastic tube he bent down and sucked the contents up, Cruel scowled at the sight as Kabbastian held his breath. Running to the middle of the chambers he immediately blew it out. The grey dust particles dispersed, flying at speed towards different scrolls like moths to a flame, when the dust connected with a scroll, it rolled from its resting place and hovered a few inches above the floor.

"What is this Aja?" Grave said becoming impatient,

"wait, be still Commander" Aja reassured. In a moment the selected scrolls floated towards Kabbastian, a large chest was brought in by the soldiers and he placed the scrolls safely inside, they then carried it away. Kabbastian stopped for a moment and hesitated at one of the scrolls, he waved his hand and could feel something pulling him from the scroll, without anyone noticing he pulled it out and pushed it into his jacket. Cruel watched Aja suspiciously as the internal building of the hill was crumbling around them, the soldiers ran to an opening in a window and waved an aircraft to escort them off the hill front. As they flew up into the dusty air the Camu hills took its final breath and collapsed into itself leaving the province destroyed and unprotected. A sonic wave swept across the surrounding areas, decaying its beauty, the trees bending with its force, the soul of the land had been taken away. Down below the refugees wandered around aimlessly, screaming and carrying what few belongings they could save. The priestess peered down at the province and smiled at her success, another wave rose into the air, but this time Aja saw a tetrahedron symbol. Her eyes opened wide with horror, as the realisation of what she has done sunk in. She had killed the feminine energy from the lands, her thoughts drifted into her past memories of the magnificence of the Camu hills and her life training as a seer she once treasured.

As they rose higher and higher, she looked out speculating whether the scrolls would now work.

"Well is the scroll in there?" Cruel interrupted Aja's triumphant but disheartened moment.

Quickly wiping a single tear, she turned towards Grave, glancing at Cruel, Grave walked towards the chest. Everyone knew that power was within their grasp; anyone of them could be in control of the planet's life force with the possession of the Autom scrolls.

The tension in the vessel was soon broken, as one of the surviving scouts flew alongside the opened door and announced what he had seen.

"What! what did they have in their possession?"

"Hmmmm, high priestess, it looked.... like... scrolls"

"scrolls, arrgh!" Aja grabbed hold of him and flung the scout off his flyer.

"Open it Kabbastian, open it!" Aja ordered.

The child crouched down and slowly opened the chest,

"feel with your heart child." Kabbastian picked up each scroll in turn and held them close to his heart.

Aja held her breath, as she waited for the child's answer.

"This one" he announced placing the scroll in the lid of the chest and continued sifting through the others.

Commander Grave paced up and down, his face now harbouring anger, waiting to hear the verdict. Cruel sat quietly watching,

"I'm not convinced we have it, something's not right" she said.

Grave peered back at Cruel for he had doubts too.

"This one and this one" the child stood up.

"There are no more of this kind in the chest, the others are enchantments."

"All is not lost we have two parts of the scroll; we can still do much with this" Aja announced.

Grave gripped hold of Aja,

"do you fool me priestess? We have risked everything for just three pieces were are the other two?" he fumed.

The priestess held his hand and slowly moved it from her throat.

"I assure you Commander, what we have will bring the other scrolls to us, one remains, not two."

"She lies Grave, I see it in her eyes, she wants it for herself" accused Cruel.

She leaped towards Aja but Kabbastian jumped between them and forced his hands forward, pushing Cruel away from his mother without touching her.

"Huh, how does he know how to do this?" Cruel was filled with rage as she rubbed her stomach from the blow.

"He is my son after all Cruel," with a brisk move Aja was nose to nose to Cruel.

"enough! enough, we must pursue the remaining scrolls I will not tolerate any more mistakes priestess" snarled Grave. Aja peered into Grave's eyes,

"did I not bring you this far Commander? Not even my husband could have done this, I can lead you to the other scroll, but you must trust me!" she soothed

"Trust you Aja, you train this boy your magic and you send your husband to war" Grave remembered that Duke was in Nu Oarren,

"yes, Aja have you heard from Duke?" he questioned

"I have been with you this hibb, I have not but I shall signal him now, guards"

The priestess turned to her son,

"take out the useless scrolls and place the two pieces in it, Kabbastian do it now." The child took the other scrolls and placed them into a cylindrical bag and pulled it over his shoulder, he then took the two scrolls from the lid and placed them back in the chest closing the lid after, the other scroll that Kabbastian had in his possession was firmly tucked away under his clothes.

"Explain Aja, who has the other scroll?" questioned Grave.

The priestess' eyes were now fixed on Cruel; she was close to foiling her plan, but Grave was too power hungry to see the truth. The priestess smiled, turning back to the Commander,

"how long did we have to wait for this moment? this is not a children's game; I have a plan. Duke will not fail, but we also need the child." Grave glanced at his wife,

"Kabbastian?" he asked raising his eyebrows

"No, no Subira's child. It will lead us to the last scroll." Grave was about to strike Aja for her arrogance when Aja continued

"I say again, all is not lost, in a few camalas the child will be born, this gives us time to prepare."

"Prepare Aja? Your next plan had better be fool proof otherwise I will deal with you myself."

"You threaten me Cruel? Oh how cruel." she bated.

"Do not mock me witch."

They stood face to face again as Grave watched Kabbastian's next move.

"Look, look" Kabbastain pointed below the craft, a flock of mabay birds flew in formation, their enormous outstretched wings allowed them to fly so gracefully across the tarred yantes skies. For a tali, silence swept the craft as they were frozen in amazement by the grandness of the sight; the long pink and white feathers parading from the mabay's plumage.

--- CHAPTER 32 ---

MOMA GOGO

Ashshun was falling over Nu Jahri, Gogo stood up from the table

"Something is wrong, sisters, sisters, sister's!" she called urgently.

The elders ran frantically into the room hearing the fear in Moma Gogo's voice. Murrock, Bakko and Junn entered close behind them. The elders guided Gogo to sit down, she wailed with pain holding onto her chest,

"she dies, she dies" she wailed,

"who Moma Gogo? Who?" asked Murrock the old woman sat limp, crippled over with sorrow

"Camu, they have broken her" the group stood bewildered by this crushing news, Queen Adama and the Empress hurried over to hold Gogo.

"They have taken away her heart" Subira held onto Gogo and lifted her head.

"Gogo what are you saying?" Lifting her head up she tried to speak through her pain.

"I saw it... I felt my contention weaken, who could have done this?" she questioned confused. The elders stared at each other for they realised that some of the scrolls were hidden within Camu,

"Moma Gogo the scrolls" one whispered. The room fell silent, no one could believe what she was telling them.

"Sisters look at the stones, quickly!" One of the elders rushed into the room, on the table the stones of Camu had darkened in colour and split in two. Her eyes were frozen in shock another line had been broken.

***

"What do you see?" Gogo shouted, the elder sluggishly wandered out of the room

"tell me!" Gogo demanded, her head raised from the loss

"they have split and darkened" replied the elder sheepishly.

Gogo fanned Subira and Adama's hands away while slowly getting to her feet

"they... split?" Gogo repeated

"We must contact Javari; we should return to Nu Oarren" Subira broke into panic and looked at both Junn and Bakko

"you go and protect your King"

"They have been ordered to be here with you Subira!" Adama stated

"Am I not the Empress of Nu Oarren? I carry the heir to the throne, I order you to go back to my King, find out what has happened to Camu." Murrock glanced at the brothers who looked anxious,

"I can protect our Empress" she reassured. Gogo sat back down and muttered,

"the season of the south land soon begins; I would not have seen it this way" the elders gathered around; holding onto each other they sobbed.

"Subira, this is not right, they should stay" Adama pleaded, the Empress ignored her mother

"Javari would want them to stay with you." Subira's tone dropped

"Well Javari is not here now! so I say go, go now!"

Queen Adama stood hurt by her daughter's commands, Bakko and Junn saluted the Empress and left; hastily followed by the Saggitta soldiers. Gogo muttered again

"More is to come. We must prepare, let Samu know our plans have changed" turning to one of the elders she said

"sister please forward a message that we will meet in the tuning chambers at ashshun fall." The sister nodded and left the room to complete the request.

Subira beckoned a maid to fetch her a chair and place it closer to Gogo, Queen Adama not knowing what to say or do after being insulted by her daughter she anxiously tried to make herself useful and left the room to get some water.

***

"Did the stones do anything? Subira looked down at them

"No, nothing, well" Gogo waited for her next answer

"earlier they were cold as I touched them individually. Gogo's head raised up from her tears,

"Good, good" Subira and the elders pondered at the joy that quickly swept over the old woman's face.

"No one but Bakko, Junn and those that dwell within these waters know you are here, my people are loyal, so you will be safe Empress" she assured them.

A faint smile crept from the corners of the Empress' mouth, as she was thinking about her and her child's safety. Gogo patted her on her lap while wiping her face with a cloth

"ahy ahy, Empress" Subira cleared her throat

"mother Gogo have we the strength to bare such a heavy burden?"

"It is your birth right, and this little one I know for sure is the key" she gently rubbed the belly on Subira

"the loss this luca is far greater than any time before, the prophecy truly unfolds" she mused.

Adama entered the room carrying a tray with fruit, cups and a jug of water. The elders left from around Gogo and entered her room to pray.

"Will we survive, do your scrolls predict this? And what of the scrolls that the elders spoke of? Were they the true Autom scrolls?" Subira asked hesitantly.

Gogo reached for a cup and poured out some water for the three of them.

"Every race thought they knew the truth, that they had the scrolls and could save our lands, we were given stories in every tongue but who's tongue speaks the sweetest notes?" she cryptically replied, both Adama and Subira looked unsure at what Gogo was trying to say.

"Are you feeling better Gogo?" Adama enquired, a small nod clarified their thoughts as she sat down Subira tenderly touched her hand forgivingly for her harsh words.

***

"I must rest for this has weakened my soul, but prayer and sleep shall fill me up again" Gogo got to her feet but she stopped momentarily in thought

"Our King will join you soon to witness the most beautiful miracle known to man and woman," her little feet totted off to join the other elders. As she opened the door, the chanting and incense burning spilled from the room; creeping into the sorrowful air. she turned back to the Empress,

"do we really carry a heavy burden? or does the weight live on all our shoulders, therefore it must be lighter" with a tiny smile she closed the door behind her.

Adama shook her head and sighed

"No matter what Subira, that old woman is full of riddles of truth, but it was hard to see her cry," Adama was filled with uncertainty but thought better than to mention it to her daughter.

Murrock stood by the entrance of the hut watching her daughter and other children playing, feeling a little uneasy she increased the armour levels on the protectors arms that were stationed around the hut, for she wanted to do her duty for the King and not let anything happen to Subira and his soon to be born child.

--- CHAPTER 33 ---

MAYHEM

Pure mayhem roared through the streets of Nu Oarren as the deafening alarms went off, protectors ran in all directions as Duke and his men surged through their defences. They triggered the explosives they planted earlier to distract the Nu Oarren army, they blasted the warlords with their stolen weapons and brought down the protective shield of the bridge. Duke and his men stormed the bridge heading in the direction of the palace and Javari. Now that the defensive shields were down Duke's flyers glided into position and blasted the army from the skies. The Nu Oarren army was despatched and Sonkel led them into battle. Javari was being dressed in his battle armour; preparing to fight with his men. Many Saggittan warriors were still in the palace grounds and assisted the protectors with holding the line. Javari signalled to Foruth,

"You know what to do, before they take us down" Foruth nodded and left the King with Dacken.

Javari commanded Dacken to lead the warlords out to the main gate, he was soon in eyesight of Duke, rays blasted from their weapons pelting down on Duke's men, but their new weapons shielded them from their missiles.

Dacken stood back astonished by the ineffectiveness of the warlord's weapons and noticed they were dressed in Saggittan armour. Duke knew their technology and had manipulated his weapons to counteract theirs. Duke and his men had manged to get into the first glass hall, maids and foot men were darting out of the line of fire. Sonkel stormed down the bridge with the protectors and fenced him in.

"You wanted us to believe you were Saggittans, your late for that lie, advance men" Dacken signalled the protectors to move forward. Surrounded by the Nu Oarren army, Duke had nowhere to go, from the pit of his stomach his shrieked out

"Ja....va...ri, I come for you!" Through the crowd of warlords Javari stood in silence, his locks bound tight, ready to fight his deceitful friend.
All weapons were pointed at Duke and his men,

"Duke. You came to take me, then do so" taunted Javari, Dacken took this as his cue and ordered his men

"Kill."

As the weapons fired towards Duke's men a crashing sound came from above, the glass shattered down in splinters they shielded their heads with their war screens. Red beams of light shot out in all directions from the crafts hovering above, blinding everyone except Duke and his men, they covered their faces with guards and were pulled up towards the crafts in seconds. Javari shouted through his monitor on his chest

"Foruth now!" near the sacred mount Foruth pushed the white crystal given to him by the King into an opening in the rocks.
Instantly the ground shook and a beam of light rose from the ground covering the entire land of Nu Oarren along with the twenty-two countries and governed by the Solomon family, only the water island could not be sealed.

As they hovered through the beam the warlords continued fire, blasting at the light. Javari ran forward

"Sonkel! Sonkel is in the light argggghhhhh!" Javari ran under the beam watching helplessly as his cousin was pulled up to their craft,

"I should have killed you Duke!" he shot repeatedly after Duke and penetrated the beam hitting Duke in his left leg.

The dome was closing fast, the noise of the crystals within its structure crackled like breaking glass, Sonkel's foot sizzled as it caught the tip of the closing sphere, they watched as he disappeared into the belly of the craft and soared up and away.

The warlords were on their flyers and up in the air in a heartbeat; shooting after the crafts, they took down two ships but were warned to not take down the craft with Sonkel in it. One protector recognised it as the same craft that took Aja and signalled the protectors to move into formation to block the craft and force it down. They surrounded the craft and used their thrusters to drive it down. Duke's pilot skilfully manoeuvred out of their grasp, higher and higher they climbed, dodging the blasts from the fire guns that were aiming to damage the engine enough to bring it down. Duke was surprised by the appearance of the dome as he had never known of its existence but was glad, they had got out when they did, even if it was a little close. They may not have won as the weapons although struck with a heavy force would not have lasted against more warlords. The beam was weaken by the amount of bodies it had to pull, he hobbled over to the cockpit and pressed the hyper speed button, it would only last for a short time but it was enough to get away, they shot out of the atmosphere and disappeared leaving nothing but smoke from its engines.

Javari stood looking up to the skies transfixed on the point where the ship had disappeared. Duke had taken his revenge, the strike didn't make any sense, they were dressed in Saggittan armour, it must have been Duke's men that stole the weapons from Saggitta.

"All of this to get into the walls, only to take Sonkel" he puzzled, Foruth joined the King and escorted him away.

The fleet scoured the skies in search of the ship but unfortunately, they were long gone. They knew there was more to come from Duke but what and when. Dacken tried to speak to him but his words were muffled as he was consumed with rage, he viewed the collateral damage of the palace, the dead men being carried off and the wounded laying along his corridors. Tormented about his wife's safety his fear rose for his cousin's life, pulling at his locks with a heavy heart he wondered how Bakko and Junn would react to the capture of their brother. As the diamond sphere glimmered over the Kingdom on lookers gasped at its magical sight, the torn King knew that war was imminent, and Duke must die this time. As they walked down the corridors Javari thought through his next steps

"Let the men retrieve any weapons and bring them to our scientists and engineers to study the technology and refine it for our army." Both Dacken and Foruth nodded as they proceeded towards the tetragon combat quarters.

"I will address the citizens in a few hibbs, we must bring calm from this."

--- CHAPTER 34 ---

PREPARATION

The tuning chambers were filled with silence, the burning incense of frankincense, myrrh, and lavender plants draped over the stones on the large hexagon amethyst table. Gogo and the elders prepared for the mourning of the Camu hills. Gogo undressed and immersed herself in the healing waters of the Goddess' of the light and truth. The weeping and whaling slowly grew within the chambers, it would be seven yantes before they were able to leave the chambers. They all knew that things would never be the same once the season of fluid law and the last law was completed, the prophecy was their only hope. Murrock was seated at the table with Nyper on her lap and some of the protectors as both Subira and Adama rested. They discussed the attack on the Camu hills and now hearing about Nu Oarren she feared the safety of the water isle land. Murrock considered whether to take the Empress, Queen

Adama and Nyper to her homeland Trigonia for greater protection.

King Javari would join them soon in a few camalas for the birth of his child, the warrior was filled with soo much anxiety she moved from the table, placing Nyper on the chair.

"You two join me outside!" she took off her armour as both protectors speculated what she wanted.

"You" she said pointing at the other protectors,

"guard the royal family with your life, if anything happens to them it will also happen to you, now come."

Standing a little way from the hut, she rolled her shoulders and cracked her knuckles

"fight me, fight me now" she challenged.

Both protectors raised their eyebrows at each other questioning her sanity, when they both looked back at Murrock they realised she was being serious. They both then stormed towards Murrock and grappled, punches and kicks were exchanged; Murrock using her sticks swiftly and artistically to defend herself against them. Not using too much force she battled with them releasing her anguish, hearing the commotion Nyper jumped down from the chair and scurried to the doorway.

Peeping her little head around the door she watched her mother with excitement. The little creature copied her mother, she twisted and spun in the air, her eyes spotting a twig hanging limp from one of the plants in a tall green vase. Her fingers pulled and tugged until she yanked it away, swirling it around her head she imitated her mother's combat moves. They fought for many hibbs until the ashshun stars were shining, both protectors sat slumped holding onto the rope bridge, exhausted. Murrock panted through the sweat pouring from her body. walking close to the men she gazed out to the sea. Pulling them up to their feet she calmly sighed

"Thank you" her eyes fell on Nyper who was flat out on the floor weakly waving her stick in the air, exhausted by the ordeal.
Murrock picked her up as her little sweaty face was grateful for the comfort of being carried,

"well done daughter" Murrock chuckled as she brought her back inside. Her training with the protectors did not change what had happened but it had shifted her troubled mood.

--- CHAPTER 35 ---

BROTHERS

As the yantes came and went, Javari's engineers worked tirelessly to master these new weapons, repairs to the first hall had almost been completed and he had addressed the citizens which brought them a sense of peace, especially with the sight of the sphere protecting them. The city was not under a curfew as Javari wanted everyone to feel safe, dozens of the warlords and protectors were in civilian clothing and moved amongst the natives yante and ashshun. The dome could last for many lucas so their defences against another attack were almost impenetrable, only the fulfilment of the prophecy could undo its strength, not even the guardian powers could bring it down. Bakko and Junn had sat within the tetragon combat quarters for almost two yantes unwashed and mourning the kidnapping of their younger brother. Their dry sweat seeped unpleasantly through the room, as they drank their sorrows away, the army steered clear from their stench. King Javari entered the quarters with Dacken and Foruth, he fanned his nose and scowled at the sight of his smelly cousins.

"Enough, get your arses up and go wash, now!" Both brothers looked down at themselves shamefully, they smelt their own arm pits; flinching from the potent odour.

Toppling chairs as they staggered to their feet, swirling half-drunk bottles in their hands, they tried pathetically to grab hold of each other to balance themselves. Slurring his words, Junn moved towards the King.

"I... am, sor... sorry Javari" hiccupping before he could finish, he breathed all over the King and tried to hug his face spilling the wine on his uniform. Junn tried to wipe away the spillage, as Javari held his arms,

"men please help them" other guards took hold of them but Bakko fought and broke free from them

"I told you, we should have killed him, now he has killed my brother." Junn spun around almost tumbling to the floor

"How... c... can you say that Bakkkko?"

"I am the eldest, so I can say what I like stupid" he chastised

"stupid... I warned you" Junn struck Bakko on his jaw and the two brothers started brawling over the table.

The guards were about to interfere when King Javari signalled them to leave them, he turned on his heels and went to the water drum. Dacken stepped forward to help the King but he shook his head indicating them all to step back.

With one big swing he hurled the ice-cold contents over the twins, they yelped like children from the shock of the cold water, sobering up the fight.

"You are an embarrassment, you call yourselves General and Officer, is this the way you conduct yourselves? You are Solomon! The blood of Solomon runs through you! Now get out and get your ridiculous selves together!" Javari twisted around and stormed out of the quarters.

"We will rendezvous in a hibb, be ready," Dacken and Foruth followed the King as he raged down the hallway, he too was troubled about the safety of Sonkel but giving into fear was not an option.

"Foruth send more warlords to Nu Jahri, pick the finest men, the best thing to happen to Subira was removing these two buffoons but Murrock needs reinforcements."

***

As the ships docked back into the belly of the large vessel, Aja, Grave and Cruel were led by Kabbastian who followed the guards carrying the chest. The priestess had received a message that Duke had the package she had sent for. Kabbastian tried his best not to let the scroll fall out his jacket, he scurried ahead of the guards to get back to his quarters quickly to hide it from their sight.

"What's wrong Son?" Aja asked, he peeped backwards

"I need the release room, my belly hurts"

"it must be all that spiritual dust, he swallowed" taunted Cruel, Aja side-eyed her as they continued down the corridor.

"When is Duke scheduled to arrive?" the Commander asked, one of the soldiers quickened his pace to fall in line with the Commander

"Around a hibb as their engines over heated, they had to take a different route sir,"

"let me know when he lands"

"Yes Commander."

With despise rattling around in Aja's heart she peered back at Grave and soo desperately wanted him out of her sight.

"Take the chest to my quarters" Grave ordered

"No! They cannot be around you, your negativity will contaminate there purity" Aja scolded.

"I don't believe the witch" sneered Cruel.

"Priestess!" Aja shouted abruptly

"Whatever, they should be near us, why don't you leave them with Kabbastian and seal them so no one can touch them." Aja's nostrils flared as she heard the glee spewing from Cruel's triumphant mouth for making the suggestion.

"Yes, yes good idea, guards follow Kabbastian and send for the builders." Lady Cruel twisted her hair in delight and sashayed victoriously past Aja who was fuming but refrained from saying another word.

Once Aja got to her quarters, she had a strong sensation and saw vision of Subira looking out to the sea watching something in the waters, it was the strongest distant sight that she had ever felt from her before especially over this time. Her stomach was filled with an uncomfortable pain, then she realised that Subira must be in pre-labour.

"Gogo must of being blocking me from the beginning or something else, I need to leave this place to see if my vision is correct, she must be in Nu Jahri, she must be this is the only safe place for her." The priestess opened her door and called for a guard, who was positioned outside of her door.

***

Each province, city and Kingdom had increased their security, the Kings of the lands planned to meet with Javari to discuss an attack on Kargel, but Grave had already made plans to move their colony out of sight leaving behind the weaker soldiers, robbers and thieves to fend for themselves. As the yantes turned into camalas, Kemi continued to spill out earthquake after earthquake, its waters raged, and many lands were swept away by the horrendous force it unleashed. Each tribe's fear deepened, that the prophecy was not true, and their fate could not possibly lay in the hands of children. This did not blind the faith in Javari's heart as he held onto the belief that something good would come from all of this loss.

--- CHAPTER 36 ---

THE PROPHECY BEGINS

Mysterious and magnificent purple and silver swirls strobed the ashshun skies as the camalas went by. The lari constellation had now moved into its first cycle, one planet was shifting into position and would be fully aligned with Kemi within four lucas. The shift created a powerful force over the planet, as the phenomenon unfolded it coincided with Subira's pregnancy, it was soon time for her to give birth. There had been no appearance of Grave, Duke or Aja, they had disappeared into thin air and after the bombing of Kargel, uncertainty still lay waiting on the mind of Javari. He sat anxiously as he and his men made their way to Nu Jahri.

Whether the citizens believed in the prophecy or not, no one could deny the supernatural occurrence that was taking place before their very eyes. The Empress was crouched as her mother gently dabbed her brow from the pearls of sweat, her contractions were progressing, it was soon time. The ashshun rolled softly into sprinkling yante, warriors waited at the docking bay for the arrival of the King. Gogo and her maids were up from early hibbs, busy preparing the royal birthing chambers near the water's edge of the Island.

The room was filled with the thick sweet aromas of the wonda plant oils, they soaked the walls and the entrance to the chambers. This ritual was practised over thousands of lucas, adding a protective healing energy at the entry of a new being helped them into their path of life. Outside the chamber's door Nyper sat comfortably on the lap of her mother Murrock, the little Tau mimicked the movement of the thin but bristly weeds with her head and tail. The warrior's bond was now instinctively sealed with motherhood and the nurturing of her growing daughter, she smiled cheerfully at the adopted child and the excitement of Adama's soon grandchild. The protectors stood outside the Empress' door ready to escort her to the birthing chambers, Subira was gently placed on a float mode, a soft bed filled of animal fur that Gogo had collected over the camalas leading up to the birth, enclosed around her body to aid and comfort her for the journey into motherhood. Gogo was surprised that the child was coming early but thought that the stress of everything could have brought on early labour. The old woman had taken the leckon bracelet from Subira that morning and handed it to Adama for safety. Her heart leapt as she looked down at the bracelet thinking about the guardians and what the fifteenth sisterhood of worshippers had told her.

As they walked along the bridge towards the birthing chambers, Queen Adama held onto her daughter's hand, the leckon bracelet glistening like small clusters of cosmic stars.

"Your husband will be here soon my love, what a glorious moment awaits him" Adama soothed.

"Mother something feels strange it feels like..." worried Subira.

Their conversation was broken by the imperial ship emerging from the water's sky, it hovered overhead, before veering off towards the docking bay.

"Ah perfect" Adama looked up smiling as she blocked the sun's rays from her eyes. The Empress followed the ship, overwhelmed with joy to see her husband after so long, the happiness quickly drained from her as the contractions came with a greater force. Gripping her mother's hand, she squeezed it tightly as Adama flinched with pain.

"Hurry" the Queen beckoned the protectors to move the craft quicker to the birthing chambers.

As the Empress moved towards the chambers, she was greeted by seven elders serenading her with a soothing ancient lullaby. Each one of their wrinkled old eyes were firmly closed, their plump bodies swished their over-sized white skirts around; fanning to the melodies. Once Subira passed them, one after another they broke their formation and followed quickly behind her but now in silence, each protector including Murrock stood back as they all disappeared into the candle lit chambers. It wasn't long before King Javari was docked and heading towards the chambers, he cautiously gazed into the bright shimmering water shield skies and from the corner of his eye he glimpsed something flying high in the air, but thought nothing of it as other traders were flying near to the royal craft when he entered Nu Jahri moments earlier. His heart was bursting with delight to see Subira and soon their child. Gogo emerged from the chambers to greet the King. Bakko and Junn walked behind him as his faithful guards Dacken and Foruth paced proudly beside the King. Murrock stood up in a command salute, Nyper joined her mother and copied her with the salute, Javari peered down at the little creature who playfully stuck out her tongue, the King giggled at the child as he entered the chamber. Murrock glared at Nyper who now had caught the tail end of the King's cloak and was marching behind him. Murrock swiftly swiped the child, lifting her clear of the cloak and into her tight embrace.

The potent scent of the wonda oil and the smouldering waves of incense was soo strong that the King staggered when it hit his nostrils. He inhaled the purifying odours which cleared his mind of the nervous thoughts. Gogo wiped his hands and forehead with more oil as he knelt beside his wife. Subira was now positioned to push as the child was crowning. Maids supported her back and wiped her forehead with cold cloths to cool her pain. The Empress listened to Gogo's instructions and took a breath for a moment. All the elders start chanting as she pushed, the mystical sounds resonated around the walls, the chambers were filled with pure love. Javari gently kissed her sweaty head, her smile faded to gritting teeth as she bared down. Suddenly a vibration moved the floor, everyone looked to the ground but thought it was in alignment of the birth. Subira screamed out and made her final push.

The ground shook more violently, soo much that the group fell to the ground, Queen Adama held firmly onto Subira. Gogo got back to her feet,

"It must be a shockwave, now push Empress. Push." There was a huge grinding sound of crumbling rocks, Subira pushed once more and before their eyes her Prince, her boy child was born.

Tears of joy flooded from Subira, before her eyes was her first-born son and her husband. Thrilling cheers surrounded the Empress, Javari's eyes were filled with tears, he could not control the love he felt for his wife and child, he gently embraced his wife as he eagerly watched Gogo and one of the elders carefully clean the child. Adama sniffled but laughed at the same time as she kissed Subira, at a snail's pace Gogo spun around flashing the tail of her skirt, the elders continued singing with praise for the prophecy child was here. Outside Murrock, Bakko and Junn laughed patting each with happiness for the King as their joy spilled out of the chambers.

The lands moved again beneath them, bracing themselves, Javari signalled that they must leave. Suddenly a thunderous crumbling and grinding sound followed by mounds of debris expelling from the ground. The chambers fell into darkness as a gush of cold sea air rushed upwards dousing all the candles. Only glimmers from the amethyst stones brought light to the darkened chambers. Once again, they were shaken to the floor, they all scrambled around to get back on their feet, Gogo covered the new-born with a blanket from the shock of the noise. The footsteps of the protectors, Dacken and Foruth echoed towards them.

"Give me my son!" Subira exclaimed, Gogo toddled blindly towards the voice of the Empress, as she reached forward and opened the blanket, the child screamed once more.

"Hurry, hurry!" Javari called.

In one swift motion something flew into the chambers, Gogo was pushed to the floor and the child was gone... Subira let out a bloodcurdling scream

"Arghhh, the pain has started again, my son." Gogo's voice bellowed into the room,

"Something has taken the child; something is in here..." Adama screamed out

"nooooooooo! The child, the child is gone, something took it noooo!" Queen Adama screamed from the pit of her stomach then fainted and fell to the broken ground, maids rushed blindly to her aid. Murrock, Junn and Bakko swarmed into the chambers, hitting upon their breast plates expelling light over everyone.

--- CHAPTER 37 ---

SEPARATION

Dusty faces full of terror reflected at them. Javari yelled and shouted orders for them to get the protectors and fly out after the assailant.

"Something has taken my child, my son, get them, get it!" Both Dacken and Foruth entered the chambers as Bakko and Junn left with haste signalling the troops as they ran. Subira kept screaming from the horror,

"my child, please no, please no aarrgghh, who has taken my child" her pain was getting worse, Gogo felt her belly and quickly moved around the bed to Subira's feet and signalled Murrock to shine the light down by the Empress' legs. The Empress screamed hysterically in a state of bewilderment and shock

"my child, where is my child?... Arrgghh, I am dying... the pain" she tossed and fought to get up from the bed, but the elders held onto her, she screamed out with a deeper pain.

"Gogo I'm dying, the pain, the pain" the old woman's face was filled with so much anger she quietly seethed to herself

"Aja... Lani-ma." She looked down at Subira and saw the emerging of another child,

"you have to push my Empress, please push" she urged.

A sorrowful gurgling and intense growl came from Subira, Gogo closed her eyes for a second and once again murmured under her breath

"the prophecy is coming forth, this is why the child, children came early."

Gogo settled herself and rubbed some oil on her dusty hands to try and clean them off before catching the child.

"Empress bare down, now push" Javari was in shock but tried his best to be calm for his hysterical and frightened wife

"Push my love push" Subira was weak but gave one strong push and the twin was born, her daughter. As she panted and sobbed to catch her breath, through the double birth and loss of her son, she started to go into shock.

"Gogo do something, do something! I cannot lose her too" wailed Adama.

An elder brought forth a blanket to swaddle the child, while Gogo waved a smelling ointment beneath Subira's nose. The scent quickly brought her around, the elder handed the baby to King Javari who was filled with sorrow but once he peered into his daughter's face, tears poured down with love. Subira kept crying as Adama tried her best to comfort her. Javari walked over to her and put their steaming daughter in her arms. As the tears fell, he wiped them away and looked at Gogo

"name her Subira, name her" Javari spoke fearfully, she gazed down at her precious daughter her shaking arms lifted the child back to Javari

"No, you name her, please name her" both Adama and Gogo looked at each other through the dancing shadows, fearing this would prevent Subira from ever bonding with her child. Javari took a deep breath

"our second born, our daughter... your mother's middle name, my mother and my sister... she will be called Kettorah Charlotte Amour Solomon" He lifted the tiny child to his face, staring into her little brown eyes he placed a gentle kiss on her tiny lips.

With a hopeless smile and saddened expression, he turned to Gogo,

"You must take them away, take them were I know not." Frantically shaking her head,

"No Javari, no... please I cannot part from you not after this... nooo" Subira pleaded. Javari exhaled a deep broken breath as Murrock stood fighting back her tears.

"Murrock look after my family, please... keep them safe, you will know when to return" The warrior bowed as the King knelt to Subira and hugged her tightly, uncontrollably sobbing through the hurt and pain as she knew this was going to be much longer than a few camalas. From all the exertion of her energy, the Empress was becoming weak but fought desperately to change the King's mind.

"Javari please don't leave me, please... I cannot." With a firm but shaky voice he looked at his wife, Adama and Gogo.

"Take them away now!"

"No, Javari... no please" wept Subira.

He pulled back from his wife, leaving a deep kiss on her lips, he then softly kissed his daughter muttering

"Kettorah you are my heart and this ashshun the prophecy has opened" He was about to leave then broke his father's protocol, he turned back and kissed Subira once more.

King Javari held his weeping wife, rage smeared cross the depths of his heart, he was defenceless but could not reveal any panic for Subira was now going into shock. Gogo summoned two elders to take Subira and the child deeper in the chambers, where she would be near the ulowpillors and the attachment islands.

Murrock re-entered the chambers in time to accompany the Empress to safety.

"Gogo" whispered Javari

"what happened? Is this not a place of protection? why has this happened?"

"hmmm" Gogo paused for a moment as the Empress left the chambers, she softy kissed the head of both Subira and her child, the sluggish body of Queen Adama walked aided by her maids.

The old women watched until they were out of sight.

"Aja knows the key to our sky; it can only be her she must have in her possession Camu scrolls. The priestess spent time here, she knows many things and was exposed to the scrolls"

"What does this mean what do I have to do to put this right, I will kill her and all that reign with her" promised Javari.

"King Javari all is not lost for two children are born and they know not of your daughter, their plan was foiled by two hearts, I did not feel the presence of two babies, the leckon bracelet blocked their energy and made them one, even their heartbeat moved as one."

"But my son Gogo, my heir to the throne, my son" the rage flew from his mouth

> "Javari, be still," Gogo's eyes widened as she looked at the King, "you must stay strong."

The Empress' elation of becoming a mother was overshadowed by painful, bitter mourning. Who or what had kidnapped her son, the heir to the throne of Nu Oarren? The warriors had now taken flight in pursuit, heading in the direction of where the strange being had flown. Protectors signalled more warriors to the chambers; they were unable to blast at the object for it carried the child into the skies. The creature soared through the skies at an alarming speed, flying high and low beneath the floating islands. Without the water shield open how could the creature get out; the creature flew through the shielding skies for a split second then it fell back through the opening, spiralling furiously out of control towards the ground. The protectors flew down and were able to scoop up the creature, they could see now that it was a Saggittan warrior, the emblem emblazoned on his right arm. He was bleeding heavily from a deep wound in his chest, the protectors sealed the wound and brought him back to the docking bay.

Guards entered the room

"My King the protectors have apprehended the invader, we have him in the healing quarters, he was a Saggittan warrior and was heavily wounded, the curers are working on extracting his memory before he dies.

"Saggittan warrior?" Javari stood instantly

"how can this be? We have an alliance with them, we must send communication to Skylan, summon the warlords and request transmission at my quarters. Take me to the perpetrator, and he came to my land for safety." Javari continued

"What of my son? Where is my son?"
The protector sadly shook his head; signifying they had not found the baby prince. On hearing this news Javari turned to Gogo,

"Gogo take Subira and Kettorah away, the King's dominant voice echoed around the chambers.

"you know what to do, tell me not where she is"
Gogo bowed she knew what was asked of her, this day the King has pronounced and exodus where he will have no communication with his wife and child until this battle is won

Javari thought of his father's teachings and all that was to come, the pain he now felt could not be hidden. Tears rolled down his face, damping his brown tunic he stood quietly staring at the heap of rocks on the ground. The King then realised a message must be sent immediately to prepare for war, his instincts felt that something bigger was coming and they had to be ready for anything after what just happened to his child. Javari handed a warrior his bead and directed him to send a distress signal straight to the warlords at Nu Oarren.

The curers fought desperately to find any information from his memory, the warrior spoke though the blood dripping from the corner of his mouth, parts of Kargel, his Kingdom were all fragmented. His distinct description was of the malevolent face of Aja and in the blurry distance, the shape of a woman with purple hair. He kept repeating Kargel, Kargel Kargel, then in a unexpected movement he sat bolt upright and chanted some ancient words he continued to repeat them until his body went into convulsion, sweat began pouring from his body, shaking violently he took one last gasp of breath, his body and blue light wings slumped motionless, his life was over.

--- CHAPTER 38 ---

DEPARTURE OF KETTORAH

Kettorah was snuggled safely in the warm bosom of her mother, unbeknown to this infant a mission lay ahead of her that would shape her dynasty forever. The elders burnt healing herbs around the Empress and guided the hover bed into the docking bay where their transport awaited them. The smoke engulfed Subira and calmed her down, the protectors and Murrock marched behind them carrying Nyper in her arms, the small creature held on to the warrior tightly as she sensed the sadness emanating from her.

Gogo emerged with the handmaids and her servants carrying baskets of food and placed them in a section of the vessel in preparation to leave Nu Jahri. King Javari was not allowed to see the departure of Subira, in case he was ever captured and the whereabouts of his family was discovered. Gogo stood at the front of the craft which lay embedded in a section of the islands. A loud shudder came up from the seas, great geezers sprayed up high into the air, the natives watched unaware of what had just happened but knew that something wasn't right after they had felt the tremor. The ulowpillor's crooning and movement had changed from soft tones and swaying to attacking the scaffolding deep below. The hatch to the craft was now closed and everyone was safely inside, its guidance system was set to one place only, Gogo held Adama's hand as they began to detach from the docking bay and slowly descended onto the sea.

The creaking timber scaffolding splintered as a small section of the island parted. Nyper scrambled out of Murrock's hands and rushed to the concealed glass dome looking out at the creatures, as they swarmed around destroying the wooden scaffolding. Some of the ulowpillors increased pace creating a whirlpool around the small craft. Shuddering their scales violently the ulowpillors pushed the craft spiralling downwards at remarkable speeds. Further and further down the craft spun down two hundred metres; its visibility from above was no more, the craft was gone.

Javari stood quietly at the edge of the docks looking out to the sea, his warriors and protectors were silent awaiting his next commands. Taking a deep breath, he signalled the men and they proceeded with Bakko and Junn. He knew this was not the time to grieve but to prepare for battle and to protect his Kingdom. Teary eyed he walked towards his cousins, pausing for a moment to revisit the feeling he had when he was seven lucas. He allowed a few teardrops to fall then wiped the heartbreak away. With another big sigh he pulled back his shoulders and proceeded to find out what was extracted from the prisoner.

***

As the ship zoomed into the skies, Aja relished over her new prize; Subira's boy. Sheer hate washed over Cruel's face as she looked at the priestess; her plan had worked, and she despised that Grave stood with her delighted by their success. In this triumphant moment, he had forgotten the missing scroll.

Kabbastian watched Cruel's movements closely and he quickly stepped in front of his mother; blocking Cruel from getting closer, Cruel was about to say something to Kabbastian but was interrupted. A message came through the speakers from Duke's men informing them that they had captured Sonkel and were returning to the new rendezvous. Aja cackled like a crazy woman and murmured

"yes, yes." Kabbastian grinned at Lady Cruel whose eyes were fixed on the priestess.

--- CHAPTER 39 ---

THE RIGHTS OF PASSAGE

The ulowpillors had long gone by now leaving the craft gliding effortlessly through the deep, deep blue sea. The underwater mounds of rock were lit up by the clusters of aquatic life, enormous multi-coloured sea urchins' and spectacular pink qway fish with beautiful plumes darted in and out of the coral reef.

The ocean's conveyor belt moved along; transparent organisms propelling themselves by discharging bursts of water, a dazzling school of amungo fish swam close to the craft, their fat blue bodies momentarily blotting out the light shining from the craft.

The passengers gasped at their gigantic size, Subira slept along with her new-born daughter Kettorah. Nyper watched timidly from the arms of Murrock as the amungo fish swam on, the craft continued to descend through a jagged split between a towering algae covered boulder.

They had been journeying for many hibbs, the water island was now so very far behind them. Downwards the craft twisted though long chiselled tunnels, it was evident that these were not a natural evolution but created by the skills of craftsmen from an underwater race. Suddenly there was a rushing of water and the craft sped up. For what seemed like an eternity the craft surged down a larger tunnel, a bellowing sound poured into the craft the water pressure had changed and Murrock looked around the vessel wondering if it could withstand the force. The craft plunged into darkness, Murrock hit her chest plate and moved into the cockpit to try and see where they were going.

Just ahead they could make out that the tunnel was getting smaller and curved sharply. They all felt a sudden surge as the craft moved through a portal and broke the surface; emerging into an enormous cavern. A dazzling light hit them, and they all covered their eyes to adjust from the darkness. Once their visibility normalised, they all looked out, the craft was dwarfed by this room, Gogo nodded to Murrock who guided a protector to manoeuvre the craft to the ocean front; they had arrived at Aqualeena the underwater city.

The roof and walls of the cavern were filled with orange stalactites and from the floor there were stalagmites that reflected against the green water. Along the water edge a figure emerged from the mouth of a cave. There stood a tall afro headed albino woman, dressed in sliver wraps of cloth and a chain from her waist holding seven circles, beside her moved a large blob of floating water.

The craft safety docked; the women moved the blob of water over the entire craft. The hatch opened and Gogo got out, as each person stepped out of craft the water sphere moved with them. As the carrier emerged holding the Empress, Nyper jumped out trying franticly to pierce the blob.

They all followed the tall women through the opening in the cavern's wall. Within the sphere a faint odourless smoke began to enter the blob. This light film decompressed the party into the atmosphere of the underground environment. As they crossed over a stone bridge, Murrock looked down and saw submerged stone structures, fossilised skeletons, the memory of a far more ancient life. As they moved along, more orbs appeared packed with different tribes of Kemi.

In front of them was a wall of a purple jelly like substance, as the sphere moved though this strange material, the blob disappeared leaving the group within a monumental palace. The woman leading them turned towards Gogo, she bent down and embraced her lifting the old woman off the ground. Gogo gave a big yell of joy as the tall woman uttered,

"Mother." with the biggest smile.

Gogo spoke softly

"Samu, my child Samu, it has been so long." Gogo's servants surrounded the tall woman and greeted her. The handmaidens, Murrock and Queen Adama stood quietly until Samu knelt to the ground bowing her head towards the vessel where the Empress lay with the princess. When she slowly lifted her head the tribe of Aqualeena materialized, thousands of her kin were all bowing.

Nyper scrambled up onto Murrock's shoulder, looking around in bewilderment at the appearance of such a multitude of people. Subira awoke and gradually sat up to see such a wonderful occurrence. The soft voice of Samu uttered,

"My Empress which energy and species."

The Empress glanced over to Gogo confused at her question. Gogo whispered into Subira's ear

"Oh, Massan people, call names energy and..." Subira stopped Gogo as she now understood the question,

"The heir to Nu Oarren throne is Princess Kettorah Charlotte Amour Solomon."

A loud noise

"dooahhh, dooooahhh, dooahhhhhh," erupted into the air startling the sleeping baby into fits of screaming, the people threw their hands up in celebrative joy.

Samu rose up and beckoned the party to move forward, as they walked through the assembly of people, they all parted to make way for the chosen one, they hugged each other with tears of joy while they continued to cheer.

The moment had come, the prophecy was born, and she was in their presence, the cheers continued rolling around the palace.

"Are the others here Samu?" Samu turned back to Gogo, her pale big brown eyes closed to gesture that the other children were there.

Nyper looked over at Samu, she could hear her talking but did not see her lips moving. Gogo looked up at Nyper whose eyes were fixed on Samu. Murrock felt the grip of Nyper's tail tighten around her neck, the warrior pulled at the creature who was now rigid with anticipation. The cheering carried on as the party moved into the imperial chambers.

The group's eyes were dazed by the sparkling chambers, thousands upon thousands of diamonds were embedded into the cave walls. Bright colourful cloth draped around the Empress' room. Murrock and the maidens helped Subira out of the vessel while Queen Adama nervously held her granddaughter, the weak hands of Subira gently touched her mother's face as she was guided by her maids to her bed.

Samu waved her hands and opened resting rooms linked to the Empress' chambers. Food had already been prepared for the warriors, protectors and the handmaidens, one of the natives invited them into a room to eat.

"I must leave you for a while my Empress" Subira nodded to Gogo as she followed Samu out of the room. Just then Nyper took sight of them leaving and jumped off Murrock's shoulder darting over to Gogo, she quickly put her hand up towards the old women.

Gogo and Samu looked down at Nyper giving her their hand as they all left the room. Murrock sat down sighing over her crazy daughter. As Gogo and Samu walked they continued talking with telepathy, Nyper could hear everything but did not understand what they were talking about or how she could now hear them this way. They boarded a shuttle and it glided off down the amazing corridors of the palace. As they came to a new opening in the caves a bubble covered over the shuttle and they ventured onto a different zone. Nyper moved around the bubble still attempting to burst it with her finger, both Gogo and Samu laughed at the fascinating child.

"Will the others be like this mother?" Gogo laughed from her belly as they floated on.

"I can only hope so, there are two, but we will talk later."

--- CHAPTER 40 ---

JAVARI RETURNS

Ashshun had fallen and King Javari was close to reaching Nu Oarren, as they flew across the provinces, they could see the collateral damage of the out skirts; burnt trees and undergrowth, cattle lay dead this planned attack had brought death to their lands. The force field shield which now covered the city glistened like stars. The royal ship slowly circled around the palace accompanied by the warrior's crafts. As they reached the main gate, an assembly of protectors stood at the mouth of the opening. The coding of their ships allowed them the fly through the dome, the DNA imprints of each resident allowed them to move to and fro safely through the dome and other cities. The ships cruised through the force field and docked in the military bay. Outside the field warlords flew around the skyline, scouting the lands.

The destruction within the palace was minimal but spoiled its exterior's beauty. No one within the walls knew about the kidnapping of the heir to the throne, Javari greeted Junn and Bakko as they departed their ship, they walked hastily in the direction of the tetragon combat quarters.

"I'm so sorry for your loss, Javari." Junn consoled. Javari looked at them both

"my loss?!"

"Our kingdom, leaving Subira, your son and Duke the Imperial Officer." Stated Bakko. There was a sudden pause and a sharp intake of breath from the King,

"Duke!"

"Ahh, yes Javari" Bakko stuttered, the King raged with anger

"then what of your brother?" Both men bowed their heads

"speak of him not my wife! After we review with the men, I believe you should both rest." Bakko replied quickly

"Aja, she is behind all of this destruction and I..."

"I only need facts, nothing but facts!" the King interrupted, they both nodded, Javari turned to Dacken and Foruth, "you both come, Bakko, Junn go rest" a frown mounted the faces of both men but they obeyed their King and walked off, annoyed at Javari's command.

As their figures disappeared down the corridor Javari whispered to Dacken

"send for the guardians and position guards near Bakko and Junn, they are restless, and I do not want them to try and do something stupid."

Dacken quickly marched off in the direction of his chosen warlords, Javari and Foruth entered the tetragon combat quarters to debrief his men and find out updates from them.

As the brothers walked towards their quarters, they debated Javari's behaviour.

"It's understandable that he is off his head, who wouldn't be? All the shame of losing this all, for some stupid prophecy." Junn shook his head at his uncaring brother.

"Pray Bakko, how would you have handled this?"

"WAR" they both said it at the same time. Junn laughed for a moment, he knew his twin so very well.

"We should go after Duke and get our brother back and I can bet he has the baby."

"Do you think Javari will let us go?"

"No, are you insane, he would not, but can he stop us if we have a plan?" Junn peered at his brother and nodded in agreement with the idea of revenge.

Something was troubling Javari and he was now becoming very paranoid of those around him, friends, family or even his guards.

There must have been other infiltrators that were feeding Aja's plans, but who? Javari's head raced catching moments of his children's birth in his mind and the painful cries from his wife. The prophecy had taken everything from him, he no longer had the comfort from his mother in-law's help through this. Surrounded by so many people he had never felt so alone.

"I must pay a visit to Kaydor, maybe they can help." The door opened and in came Dacken carrying a message,

"your highness we have sent a signal, but nothing sent back." Javari seemed shocked

"what, what is going on? We can always make contact with them, always." Clenching his hands together he thought more deeply about everything. The room went silent, all the men and women's faces stayed focused forward not to offend the King, for they could hear from this tone he was now unsure.

"We must keep the utmost dignity and honour with our fellow kingdoms, for we know not who else is against us, but we must remain in alliance with who stands as our allies." Javari rose from the chair and all the warriors stood up after him.

Dacken and Foruth escorted the King out of the room, a slight look between both bodyguards indicated that they too were worried for their King. They knew he was grieving and would do anything to protect him. As they passed the bowing servants down the corridor, Javari just wanted to shout from the pit of his stomach. All the lucas of training and hope for the end of their planet's destruction was taking its toll. Their kingdom held the last written account of the prophecy, he had never imagined this outcome. But he also knew, if it was going to take eighteen lucas he would not give up seeing it through.

--- CHAPTER 41 ---

THE STOLEN PRINCE

The ashshun had fallen and the ships docked into the larger vessel that was housed in their new location; the abandoned Sekoru fortress, its old mines were uninhabited after many lucas of earthquakes, leaving the structure too dangerous to mine. With the craftsmanship of Grave's engineers, they were able to adapt Sekrou into their new hiding place. Aja walked hastily into the lift carrying the baby followed by Kabbastian, Lady Cruel and Commander Grave. Anger had silenced Cruel as she stared at the child wondering how she could turn this prize into her own victory.

"One of my slaves has bred, she will feed the child, my Commander." The priestess quickly responded to Cruel's request.

"Fine, but she will stay in my quarters," Aja glanced back at the now furious Cruel, whose teeth gnashed at Aja's shift of power again.

As they emerged from the lift they were greeted by a hobbling Duke, his left leg now covered in a metal cast from the wounds of the attack on Nu Oarren. Aja didn't pay him any attention but stayed focused on the baby.

He looked down at the new-born and the loving aura resonating from his wife. His thoughts pondered on how he could use this hidden joy to his advantage. He stood near Grave as Aja walked on towards her quarters,

"summon the slave Cruel, bring her to my quarters, this child needs feeding and a good bath from all this after birth." Cruel's nostrils flared in disgust, her brow wrinkled into ridges and her lips tightened to hold back her rage.

Her eyes met with the Commander's for a tali, stepping towards the priestess, quickly noticing her fury he held her wrist pulling her back and whispered,

"in time, my love." Her anger slowly faded from her face as his grip relaxed. Kabbastian caught up with his mother, then held onto her gown following her to the chambers.

"We must discuss Commander, our invasions of tactics, and build our army up," Duke stood behind Grave and Cruel overhearing their conversation.

"Come then" the Commander pointed towards the war room as Cruel walked off down the corridor to her slaves.

Aja entered her room and placed the sleeping child upon her bed, she softly smiled at the infant. Her power-hungry mind was torn by the inner spirit of motherhood, Kabbastian was a useful tool but to see this new-born echoed feelings for a moment that soothed her broken soul. Her memories flashed to and fro from holding her own lifeless son to this miracle of existence now asleep in her room. Kabbastian interrupted her by announcing that the slave had arrived.

A Tau woman was at the door panting from running in fear not to keep the priestess waiting. The cowering slave was ushered into the room and directed to sit on a chair in the corner.

"When he wakes feed him, what is your name?"

"Wone, priestess."

"Wone? Is this your tribe's name?"

"Yes priestess." Aja thought for a moment

"well Wone, make sure this child is fed and kept as your own suckling child, be with him at all times, this is your job and only this." Wone's head bowed with sadness,

"my priestess, for who is to suckle my own child if I am to become a wet nurse for this child, can I do both?" Aja stormed across the room and slapped Wone across her face, she yelped from her fiery hand.

"You dare to speak of your offspring, this is royalty, royalty, some other animal will feed it," Kabbastian flinched when Aja hit the slave and naturally moved over to the baby to protect him. The smart child quickly changed the mood in the room,

"what shall we call him mother, my brother?"

"Hmmm," the priestess cupped her face and walked towards the bed.

She sat next to Kabbastian pondering for a moment,

"he is a prince is he not? Then, so then he shall be Prince Toreon."

Kabbastian glared at his mother, she had never called him a prince and from that yante he knew she would never care for him the same way.

"Wone clean him for he smells of birth, do this now."
Wone left to fetch water and towels to bathe the child, Kabbastian moved closer to the baby, staring down at Prince Toreon, he stroked the baby's forehead with one of his fingers now despising its presence.

Cruel was up on the top deck watching Aja's movements, she had fastened a spy camera within the necklace of the Tau slave, in the palm of her hand she held a device and viewed the Tau washing the baby while Kabbastian observed. Aja was out of sight, but she knew now the power was truly in the hands of the priestess and she had to overthrow her dominance and find a way to take control of Aja's position.

Duke limped his way across the room to stand at the window now looking out to nothing but rocks,

"when shall we deploy for our next invasion?"

"We wait, we still need that final scroll, this child shall cripple the strength of King Javari, or it will thicken his heart, I hope it is the latter."

Duke watched Grave moving holograms of his small army around the Kemi map.

"Eighteen lucas is a long time of war to seize power of Kemi and its tribesman, but I shall wait, and nothing will stop me, nothing!"

Duke sipped from a goblet; this shift of universal power would not only change Kemi but galaxies away would be in oppression over a thousand lucas with the possession of the Autom scrolls. Grave needed the battle tactics of Duke's knowledge, although he was a sinister man, he knew only a little of how to truly control a large army.

"Then together we shall build a new force, one that will seize the power and we will reign as rulers."

"Rulers?" he smirked at Duke's words and continued moving the army to uncharted territory. As his hands continued separating his men into groups, he remembered the planet he had come from. His planet was many lucas away, he had escaped the prison of Rezone Mountain and heard of this world and its power. The commander was once a destitute man, his planet was dying, and his family were taken as prisoners to other distant planets. He was left with many other children to live amongst the criminals and thieves. He was able to escape this planet by stowing away in a craft navigated by a malevolent gang of unlawful convicts; they joined together to thieve, kill and destroy for survival. He grew in the ranks, receiving a tattoo on the left side of his neck to state his rank and commitment to the gang. He impressed them by his tactics and intuition and soon had his own ship to command.

As he was about to leave a barren planet, it was there that Grave met Lady Cruel, she was scarred from her own past, but she thrived on the pain. Her beauty was covered by her conning manipulation techniques of survival. Only one person could ever break her harden armour and Commander Grave was the one to do this. He captivated her with his grey blue eyes and his hunger for power. Cruel begged Grave to take her with him which he agreed, with one request that she would become his wife.

They made an alliance and began overthrowing each gang member. Their thirst for power grew as they travelled to many quadrants and heard many stories about a distant galaxy holding a frequency of light. They searched for more information of this tale of a planet and scrolls that would give supreme governance over the universe to its possessor. This was something that they were waiting for, this they thought would give them the respect they sort after.

This crew of barbaric men and women had collected enemies from all over the universe and it wasn't long before the gang were captured. They were all banished to the mixed prison of Rezone Mountain. Grave and Cruel along with two other men were able to escape their ninety lucas imprisonment. It was there within in the walls, a tribesman from Saggitta had fled after the war with King Agu. He got caught up with careless invaders and was soon captured and imprisoned for his crimes. He traded the co-ordinates of the planet Kemi with Grave after bargaining his safety once they escaped. After they got away, the Saggitan man was greeted by the blade of Cruel. They voyaged for three lucas to find the galaxy that housed planet Kemi. Grave was not fearful of waiting for eighteen lucas as his prison sentence would have been far greater, if he could have within his grasp the power that could cripple any planet he would wait, for him, time was not a problem at all.

Duke started to move pieces into position on the map, the territories that needed to be captured, he thought that the force field would possibly weaken each yante. Despite the alliance between Saggitta and Volker, Grave knew small fractions were against Javari and he would stand with them to become their comrades.

"We must take the poorer clans, the outcasts and criminals to be trained and fight beside us." Duke knew this was music to Grave's ears, they both moved the pieces together on the map,

"yes, yes that sounds like my sort of plan." Duke looked into Grave's eyes and raised his goblet waiting for Grave to join him in a cheer to victory, but the commander did not, he just stared back at him with a crooked smile.

--- CHAPTER 42 ---

CONNECTION OF THE CHILDREN

Gogo sat on a small stool surrounded by a thick circle made from gold, she placed a bowl of ban roots next to her, while Nyper curiously stepped into the circle. Within a blue coloured room all the evacuee children from the different cities were now gathered. The royal children were quickly separated from others and were ushered into the room where Gogo awaited. Nyper and Gogo watched the children enter the room, each one was asked to sit on a specific cushion within the circle. The prince and princesses from, Aqualeena, Volker, Gep, Saggitta, Colwaya and Aceda all sat, they gawked at other wondering why they were placed in the circle.

Samu nodded to Gogo as she stood up and walked slowly around the children, each child turned as she passed them handing them a yellow gem. As she went back to her seat, Gogo picked up Nyper who was enjoying her ban-roots and whispered into her ear. The creature's eyes widened as she listened carefully, her quiet voice repeated back to Gogo just to be sure. Nyper then jumped up and began to scurry around the children.

"Up right Nyper" shouted Gogo.

The creature nodded then stood up and walked more slowly, she passed each child sniffing the air around them.

Eventually she stopped she looked at the Volker child and pointed at her, Princess Sundella sat up more confidently and glanced at the other children. The creature than went along back and forth until she stopped again and pointed one more time, at the Saggittan Prince Ulen. Nyper walked back to her seat smiling from cheek to cheek, feeling successful from her task.

"The rest of you beautiful children may go back into the other blue room, but my prince and princess please follow me." They all rose, the two children followed Gogo with Samu and Nyper behind her.

They walked along the pale peach crystal corridors until its textured faded into glass. Huge bubbles moved along the outside of the glass almost following their direction. Nyper glanced around the space as she was led to a large silver door. Samu unlocked the door and before them were positioned five small silver pods and surrounding them were five larger gold pods, one at a time Samu took each child and lifted them to sit in the pods,

"What is this for? you all trying to kill us, you better have another plan otherwise..."

Sundella opened her hands preparing to attack Samu, Ulen looked over at Sundella agreeing with her concern.

"No," the soothing voice of Samu calmed their fears away.

"None of you will come to any harm this is part of your destiny, you are all gifted for this reason, Nyper chose you, come Nyper you too must rest."

The creature frowned reluctantly and moved towards the pod that Samu was pointing to. As she jumped up and sat on the soft bed Samu gave her a yellow gem, a gentle mist seeped down from the top of the pods covering over them all. Gogo spoke softly

"We need you all to rest now, for your journey has just begun," Samu gently guided their heads to lie down. Nyper fought hard to keep her eyes open as she watched the pod case close over them.

Samu placed her fingers in grooves positioned at the top of a much smaller pod in the centre of the circle. As she closed her eyes a beam of light pulsed towards the other pods and moved up and down the bodies of the children. A small probing needle appeared from the inside of the pod and took a sample of each child's blood. Samu's temples began to glow a pale pink colour. The pod then became immersed with a yellow light reflecting from the gem which the children still held onto. Once the sequence of toning was completed Samu opened her eyes while removing her hands and her temples stopped glowing.

Samu bowed towards Gogo,

"their merging is complete," before their eyes the chosen ones where preparing for their destiny.

"Mother, Murrock and Kettorah then it is completed." Samu gazed down at Gogo kissing her on her forehead, they then left the room and headed back to the party.

--- CHAPTER 43 ---

THE RISE AFTER THE FALL

The Empress was now awake and nursing her daughter, Queen Adama sat beside her smiling at the sight of the joy on her daughter's face. Murrock was eating at the table with the five warriors and three handmaidens; this was the first time in a long time that the warriors were truly relaxed from their duties. Murrock glanced over at the Empress with a subtle smile, as she saw peace wash over her face as she fed her daughter. As strong as she was, Subira's thoughts weighed heavily over the abduction of her son. Her eye's scanned over Kettorah's face imprinting every part of her character.

"I see Javari's forehead"

"hmmm" Adama smiled and moved closer to her daughter and viewed over her beautiful granddaughter.

"Here, my child," Adama handed back the leckon bracelet to Subira,

"Once Kettorah is twelve lucas she is to wear this." The Empress carefully held the jewels then placed it into her gown pocket.

"Why is this so important now mother?" Queen Adama took a deep breath,

"I was given this at the fold of Aluke," Subira looked at Adama in shock,

"when were you at the fold of Aluke?" Adama side-eyed her then continued,

"I witnessed a battle, but I cannot be sure who was fighting, Adama was not telling Subira everything.

"The bracelet took my memory away, but I knew that I needed to give it to my child, and then for them to do the same. I was given a message of five hearts, wars that bring peace, and... the end, this is the key to the end." Subira stared into her mother's eyes,

"end? Mother what end?" Adama looked back to the infant now peacefully sleeping.

"Do you mean my children's lives?"

Subira could not contain herself anymore, overcome with emotion she fought back her tears

"I cannot spare this ache in my heart mother, my son! You talk of this leckon bracelet, and battles, what about my children's safety?" The Empress' eyes filled with tears,

"mother what of my son, did you know this would happen to him, he could be... this is too much to bare! How can I now possibly continue to feel love for her while I truly cry inside for my son too?" Subira gasped for air as her temper rose,

"She suckles pain from my breast! Mother, pain!"

"Subira!" the Queen spoke abruptly, an awkward silence fell in the room,

"It is your duty, and you must not allow worry to engulf your soul, I understand this is so much to bare but..."

"How can I possibly face all of this with no proper direction, I cannot do this mother I cannot, and what does this bracelet have to do with my child's life now?" Murrock peeked up from her plate, hearing the distress of the Empress.
Subira glared at her mother, then took the bracelet from her pocket and threw it across the room.

"You could never understand mother, never! And that, what good, was it to me, for it did not save my son! Nor, did Gogo Amakia!" Adama

looked at her daughter's vexed face while glancing where the bracelet had landed.
Disappointed by Subira's words she walked over to retrieve the bracelet and summoned one of her maids over. Slowly under her breath she muttered

"you have no idea my child."

Her thoughts raced around, and she knew what she had to say and do to strengthen her daughter. Filled with tears she spoke through a quivering voice.

"Treasure this moment Empress, worry no more put your spirit into balance, moan, scream and cry if you have to, but this child needs you! Empress you must, you must now be stronger than you have ever been in your life and take your throne this is the imperial way." Subira looked up hearing the seriousness from her mother's voice, she called her Empress.

"I give you three camalas, three, and once you return you must prepare." Adama looked over to Murrock, the warrior nodded at Queen Adama for she knew what was coming next.

The maidens and other warriors in the room looked quickly up towards Queen Adama, those words 'imperial and calling Subira Empress' they had never heard before. Adama always called her Subira but now her mother's tone had changed. From that day forth Adama would never call Subira's name again, she took a deep breath for she knew what was to follow. Adama stood up and walked towards her belongings; she rustled through her bags and then took out a ruby ring.

This ring was her wedding ring, it should be only given to Subira after the death of the Queen, Adama knew this could be the only way to strengthen her daughter's pain and duty. As she wiped her tears away, she buried her emotions as well as her title. Her maid carried over Adama's purple royal ribbon decorated with both family's seals. As she placed it into Adama's hand, Gogo stepped through the door and stopped as her eye caught sight of the ring, this was the imperial order she had seen once before, Samu and the old woman stood quietly until the conversation had ended. The room went silent, Murrock spun around to see where Nyper was and Samu lifted her hand, signalling to Murrock that she was fine.

Murrock, the warriors and handmaidens all got up, Queen Adama walked closer to her daughter, she ushered a maid to hold the child.

Stand my Queen, Subira burst into floods of tears and sat back down

"Mother, what are you doing?" She knew that Adama was denouncing her title as Queen Mother to give Subira her full birth right.

"You don't have to do this! Please mother, please!" Adama would now become, her daughter's imperial scribe, documenting, her Royal Highness' duties and daily accounts and the children, and sadly her mothering duties.

Adama knew this was the only way to give her daughter that final surge of power, she was now a Queen from birthing her twins, but denouncing her title would make Subira clear of how serious this was and how she needed to be ready. Adama knew that, if she ever sank into a deep depression from the loss of her son, both mother and child would surely perish. The Queen pulled Subira to her feet, and placed the leckon bracelet in her hands, words were exchanged quietly in her ear and then Adama knelt and bowed seven times, as she did so, everyone followed suit. Adama took off Subira's wedding ring and placed it on her right hand, then placed her ring on Subira's wedding finger. After the exchange

Adama said "hail to her Royal Highness Queen Subira, they all addressed her,

"Hail Queen Subira of Nu Oarren, hail to our Queen."

Subira took a large gulp and reluctantly addressed them,

"Rise my faithful subjects." The new Queen kept her head held high to avoid looking directly at her mother, Adama got up and then said,

"Our Queen requires three camalas of mourning, let this be so," she bowed again and then left the room to her chambers.

Tears flooded from Adama's face as she closed the door behind her, the pain gripped her stomach and she curled into a ball sliding down the door to brace her fall, she had no choice but to do this. Subira had to become stronger to face the war ahead, the spirit of warrior-ship must be called upon, this was the only way. Adama knew that trauma brought weakness, so she had focused her pain into power.

Gogo looked deep into Queen Subira's eyes, fighting with her might not to cry.

"Maids, preserve milk for three camalas, take your Queen, we will leave in three hibbs." Unhappiness fell over Samu as she glanced at Gogo; they then sat with the old woman as she explained to Murrock what was to happen next.

--- CHAPTER 44 ---

BINDING OF BLOODS

The hibbs passed and Queen Subira was taken to a craft only Murrock and Gogo accompanied her. Samu cradled Kettorah, the handmaidens and the warriors went back to the pods. Samu called Murrock aside and extracted some blood from the warrior's thumb before they all departed.

Samu carried Kettorah to where the other children lay resting, she was then placed into the small pod in the centre. As it closed Samu placed the blood into a chalice, the chalice was then placed in a hatch in the small pod. From the ground, tubes rose up and connected all the pods. This process was the joining of the house of Kemi, bringing order and alignment of spirits. Once the pod that held Kettorah started pulsing the blood from all the children flowed to the container then straight to Kettorah's body. The infant cried out as the transformation commenced. As each bloodline combined with hers, her facial features underwent an advanced metamorphosis until her appearance went back to a normal hue. Samu walked around looking into the pods checking over each child, she nodded as things were progressing accurately. As there was no rejection by Kettorah, the combination of bloodlines was the next vital stage of the prophecy. Samu walked over to the container and peered to see the blood gone and now there was water. The door to the container was opened and Samu extracted the water into a small vile.

***

Gogo kissed Queen Subira on her cheek,

"Kettorah shall be brought to you" the old woman paused looking into the Queen's eyes

"your mother is still your mother; this will never change." Biting her quivering lip, Subira nodded with a faint smile,

"I need my mother now Gogo, not some silent scribe!" The old woman sighed

"look after her Murrock,"

"yes Gogo." Murrock nodded.

With the aid of a Masson woman they boarded a craft bound for a sacred space in Aqualeena for the Queen to mourn peacefully.

In returning to the room Gogo searched for Adama, one of the handmaids pointed to a door. Gogo totted over to it and opened the door slowly, she had to force it to open as Adama was behind the door,

"Adama! Let me in" Still on the floor Adama shuffled from blocking it.

"Gogo," a weak voice fell from her lips

"can you give me something to help me to sleep old lady" Gogo nodded,

"hmm, give me a moment." The old woman wondered off then came back with a pipe,

"we have a little time, come." Gogo guided her to another room away from the group, the old woman lit the keba powder pipe and handed it to Adama. Adama closed her eyes leaning her head back against a chair,

"Have I done the right thing? Did I do this too soon?"

"What, too soon, pull on the pipe with your dry lips?" giggled Gogo

They both chuckled and then burst out in fits of laughter, to which Adama laughed herself into floods of tears, Gogo held her as she cried for her daughter. She pulled from her pocket a rough cloth to wipe her tears,

"Do you want to rip my skin Gogo?" A smirk rose on the old woman's face

"better than ripping your heart." Adama sniggered through her tears and then started to laugh again,

"I do love you woman." The snorting and bellowing laughter spilled out from the cracks of the door floating to the ears of maids and warriors, they chuckled along with Gogo and Adama hearing a little happiness amidst so much pain. As the laughter slowly subsided Gogo turned to Adama

"your heart knew it was time, and we cannot fight what is in your heart it was the right time,"

"it just hurt to see her face; it was if I died in front of her." The old woman gently smiled as she touched Adama's arm,

"but you're surely not dead at all, but you will sleep, yes you will sleep." Nodded Gogo knowingly.

***

Subira was now dressed in a pink silk robe and wandered around the space, it was a calming environment filled with reflective lights, yellow hanging sea weeds and soothing music surrounding the air. It was her solitude for a moment, an isolated void to sink her anger. Still overcome by everything that happened in that yante, she rambled around aimlessly. Her eyes gazed at the ring, then she collapsed to the floor and with all of her might she screamed and screamed out the pain inside. The imprint of her son's face kept haunting her mind and not being able to see her love, Javari.

"My son!" she sobbed,

"is gone… my first born, I cannot even feel the warmth from my husband's arms through this pain Murrock, this torture! How can I bare this and now my mother! My mother, I have no mother! How do they all expect me to cope through this? I am but flesh Murrock, I am but flesh, my child." Falling to the ground she pulled heaps of grass out while her body quivered in silence.

Her eyes glanced the bracelet that was half falling out of her pocket, grabbing hold of it she threw it as far as she could. Murrock looked to see where it had fallen and would retrieve it later. Queen Subira cried and screamed until she made herself so weak that she fell asleep. Murrock carefully picked her up and carried her to the resting area, she felt so much sadness for the Queen and had a secret moment to shed a tear.

Samu and her kin had now brought the children from the pods and guided them to their sleeping quarters. Carrying the infant, she handed her over to the nursing maid, the glass vile was now around Kettorah's neck.

"Where is Gogo?" A maid explained what had taken place and pointed to the door where they both were.

Samu then looked towards the door sniffed a little and allowed a tiny snigger

"Let the Queen sleep for one ashshun and then bring her the child

END OF PART ONE

Keep your ears and eyes peeled for the next instalment of Kettorah and the Autom scrolls of light coming Summer 2020

IF YOU CAN'T WAIT THAT LONG HOP ON TO THE WEBSITE BELOW:
WWW.KETTORAHPART1.COM

Acknowledgements

I am thankful to the creator, for gifting me with the art of creative writing. To my beloved parents Viris and Leonard Carter, I am so thankful for your encouragement that allowed me to explore my imagination and creativity. To my brothers Paul and Gauntlet Carter, thank you for laying the foundations of my love for fantasy stories and comics. To Joy Whilby thank you for your encouragement and believing in me, to write this series and more. Thank you to my accountability partner Richard Williams, and John Morrison of Nurvax arts productions, for investing in me. Thank you to my Ana rap crew, for without our Friday nights of free-styling Mc sessions, Kettorah, would never have been born. Blessings to Samantha Clarke, Petula Clarke, Jennifer Hemmings, and Gillian Harvey. To Minister Kelly and the members of the former church of the Redeemer thank you for your guidance. To E Double D, Janet Douglas-Gray, Jasmine King, Andrea-Baker-Reid, Yvonne Williams, Marcia Spence, Paris Walker, Leonie Smith, Natalie Flanders, Alison Johnson, Chantelle

Reid, Winsome Duncan, Rachael Cox, Michael Henry, Juice-Aleem, Ian-Jamo-Campbell, Leo Purvis, Paul Snook, Amelia McMahon, Lauren Hoyle, Pam Rayment, Salma Akhtar, Sam Darley, Meg Houston, Siobhan Harper-Nunes, Cheryl Garvey of Shakti woman, thank you all for reminding me to reach beyond the stars.

To sensei Chris Hamilton thank you for wisdom, guidance, support and your mad skills. To Samantha House thank you for seeing my vision through and reminding me not to 'peer' too much. To all my family, friends, colleagues, young people, my Hip Hop family, fellow nerds, dyslexic's warriors and geeks, thank you for supporting my dreams, with love and positive vibes. To Jean-Pierre De Villiers, thank you for my 'why and why not.' To Errol Lawson, Alex Rozwalka Attebey, Des O'Conner, Selina Brown, Dr Christopher Johnson, Dr Martin Glynn and Lucy Mair, for sharing your knowledge and guidance on this journey. To Eric Thomas, Damon Dash, Lisa Nicholls, Gary Vaynerchuk, Tom Bilyeu, Patrice Washington,

John Gary, T D Jakes to name a few, whom have kept me going through challenging times. Thank you to the late great Toni Morrison for reminding me that if there is a story that you want to read and it is not out there, 'write it.' To all my angels, those who are no longer here with us, thank you for inspiring me to go for it, and to never take anything for granted. They echo a beautiful prompting melody, that this is so much more than a story, it's a movement of love.

Forever thankful.

***

About the author

Sandra. E. Carter, born and raised in Birmingham UK, her avid love and passion for the creative arts, has enabled her to support the development of many young people's lives, by continually encouraging them to pursue their dreams. From fashion to dance to music, each art form enabled Sandra to express herself, but her love for writing outweighed them all. Writing allowed her to stretch and explore her imagination leading her to give birth to an amazing fantasy series. Having a burning desire to overcome the stigma of the disability 'dyslexia,' Sandra embarked on creating a new voice for those who may feel embarrassed or ashamed of being dyslexic. Being a huge fan of anime, manga, fantasy and sci-fi, she let go and disappeared into her imagination, immersing herself into the world of Kettorah. Then one day, on a chilly winter evening the 5th November 2018, she looked up and had written three books and counting.

'This has been a labour of love, one of which I am truly, truly grateful for'

\- *Sandra E. Carter*

Amen

Printed in Great Britain
by Amazon

32516201R10219